HURT SO GOOD

A Break So Soft Novel

STASIA BLACK

Copyright © 2019 Stasia Black

ISBN-13: 978-1-950097-11-1
ISBN: 10: 1-950097-11-0

All rights reserved. No part of this publication may be reproduced, distributed, or transmitted in any form or by any means, including photocopying, recording, or other electronic or mechanical methods, without the prior written permission of the publisher, except in the case of brief quotations embodied in critical reviews and certain other noncommercial uses permitted by copyright law.

This is a work of fiction. Similarities to real people, places, or events are entirely coincidental.

CHAPTER ONE

DYLAN

I stare over the rim of my glass of bourbon, watching the bombshell in the red dress work the room.

She's good, I'll give her that.

She flirts just enough with the men—only the important ones, I note—a touch of her hand on their shoulder, the brush of her hip, the flash of her smile. She's making them feel like they've gotten something from her but then she moves on before they can really get a taste.

And the more I watch her, a taste is exactly what I want of the woman.

I don't even know her name but my cock has been stiff for the last half hour as I've nursed my bourbon and watched her.

This is a bullshit mixer the Silicon Valley Robotics Symposium puts on every year, and it's made exactly for this kind of shit. To encourage the greasing of wheels that actually gets deals done. An open bar. A tight red dress. A word or two in the right ear.

The hotel ballroom is dimly lit while a band plays soft, unremarkable jazz on a small stage up front. Meanwhile, middle-aged men with flushed faces laugh too loudly at jokes and are a little too obvious about their hopes for getting laid. Because it's a tech conference though, there are about two guys to every woman, so their chances aren't good.

And then there's her. The woman in red.

I wonder what company the woman represents.

It doesn't matter. You aren't going to find out and you sure as fuck aren't getting a taste of her.

I frown and tip my glass back, draining the last of the bourbon. Don't know why the fuck I even stopped by here after my presentation. My brother, Darren, kept saying I needed to at least show my face or it would look rude after I gave the keynote speech. Considering he's also my business partner, I thought, *fine, I'll drop in for a few minutes and then get the hell out of here.*

Until I saw her.

Trouble is what she is. Trouble I don't need.

Which is why you're leaving. Right now.

I stand up and put the glass down on the bartop, then turn and—

Almost run straight into her. *Her.*

"Where you off to in such a hurry?" She flashes the same mega-watt smile she gave every other guy in the room and my eyes narrow. She thinks she's gonna run her game on me? It's insulting. Do I look like all the other desperate fucks in here?

I ignore her and reach for my coat and umbrella, then I move again to leave. I don't step around her, though. I step into her and our bodies do more than brush. We collide and I hear her quick intake of air as she rocks back on her heels.

I expect her to get pissed at the dick move. Which is for the best because I just need to get the hell out of here. Discipline has been my watchword for the last six years and I'm not about to blow it now.

But when I glance her way, her posture is completely different.

Her eyes have dropped to the floor and her head is bowed. Submissively. Her brunette hair shines in the dim light of the wall sconces and now that she's here up close I can see that she's younger than I first thought. Maybe only twenty-five? Twenty-six?

And then I see her tongue swipe out to lick her lips at the same time her chest heaves, ample cleavage rising and falling dramatically.

I'm captured by the sight and when a moment later she glances back up at me, the lust is clear in her eyes.

Who the fuck is this woman?

"Who are you?" I'm not a man who beats around the bush.

"Miranda Rose. With ProDynamics. And you're Dylan Lennox of The Lennox Brothers Corporation."

My eyebrow lifts. ProDynamics, huh? Rod Serrano, the CEO, has already put in his bid to have their Pro processors in our newest robotics motherboards we're pushing out. He keeps calling to get updates about his bid but I've been ignoring his inquiries.

Is putting this siren in my path his latest attempt to sway me into taking a meeting with him?

"Wow. Rod really does go all out," I sneer. Rod will find out along with everyone else when we make the announcement of which processing chip we're going with. But I already know I'm not interested in his processor. Processors like Intel has capitalized on—and like ProDynamics keeps producing—are the past. I'm more interested in the future.

The woman's eyes flare but she doesn't say anything. Fuck. She doesn't look pissed by my asshole attitude. She looks turned on. And her lust seems genuine.

Or she's just one hell of an actress.

Either way, no fucking way I'm letting my dick have any say in my business dealings. Jesus but I learned that the hard way, didn't I? I barely survived the scandal last time and only because I had the money to pay to make it go away quickly.

Never again.

So no matter how luscious Miranda Rose looks in that red dress and those fuck me heels, I continue pushing past her. My eyes shut briefly as I inhale her seductive scent but then I'm finally away from her.

I stride for the door and *almost* make it.

A red-faced Ken Kobayashi stops me feet from the door, clapping me on the back. "Dylan! Good to see you! Loved your talk. Come, have a drink with us." He gestures toward his table of big wigs from the Japanese tech sector who flew in for the conference.

I force a smile and shake him off. "Sorry, I'm heading out."

"No, man, you gotta come hang." Ken grew up in the states and we briefly knew each other in college. He's the opposite of every Asian stereotype—he always loved partying instead of studying, barely got by in his classes and only managed to get the position he has now because his daddy pulled strings for him in the family company.

Over his shoulder, I see Miranda heading out of the hotel ballroom, ass swaying sinfully in the red dress.

My cock stiffens again. Fuck, I need to get out of here and get home where I can take myself in hand and give in to all the fantasies crowding my brain before I embarrass myself in public.

"Great seeing you, Ken," I cut him off mid-sentence. I clap him on the back and then head out the same door she just left through. She's only about twenty feet ahead of me, strolling with those hips still swaying through the lobby and out a side exit to the garage.

I'm not intentionally following her.

... I don't think.

I'm just making sure she gets to her car safely. She'll never even know I'm here. It's the gentlemanly thing to do.

As if I could ever be accused of being gentlemanly. I know what this really is.

Just more fuel for tonight's fantasies.

For once, I'm giving in to the rush of what it feels like to stalk my prey.

CHAPTER TWO

MIRANDA

My heels click clack on the stairs as I head up to the third floor of the parking garage.

Hairs tingle on the back of my neck, the same way they always do when I walk anywhere at night in the city.

It's not safe to be a woman alone.

The thought both thrills and terrifies me. Because I'm fucked up. I'm a seriously fucked up woman.

I bite my lip at the thought of the man in the bar.

Dylan Lennox.

His chiseled face and broad shoulders. Those eyes that captivated even as they dismissed me.

The man who followed me out of the hotel into the garage.

I don't hear his footsteps on the stairs behind me, though. Will he take the elevator? Or was he not following me after all?

He was leaving, too. He's probably just heading to his own car.

But he's Dylan Lennox. Surely he used valet parking.

I bite my lip as I reach the top of the staircase. I only offer one glance over at the elevator before pushing through the door to the open air of the top floor of the garage.

I parked at the very end of the row, at the corner of the rooftop. As I go, I force myself not to look back like I usually would. It's dark and I'm a woman alone. I'm supposed to be afraid.

And my breaths do come quicker with every step I take. I hurry, almost at a jog or as near to as I can in these heels.

My heartbeat only calms once I reach my car. A red Corvette, naturally. I'm so careful about the packaged product I want to project to the world as I make myself up each morning. The Corvette is all part of it.

Confident. Sexy. Desirable.

In control.

Everything I wish I actually was.

I reach in my tiny clutch purse and pull out my key, ready to push the button to open the door—

When I'm pushed from behind, my face crushed into the glass of the driver's side window.

"Spread your legs, bitch."

It's not Dylan.

The breath is heavy with the stench of cigarettes and the arm that cinches around my neck is merciless.

I let out a small cry before the arm tightens around my neck.

A foot kicks my legs apart. My ankle turns at the rough movement and I cry out again but it doesn't matter.

Nothing matters to the man at my back as he rips my dress up to my waist. I'm not wearing underwear because the dress was so tight that even the strings of a thong would have shown.

I cough and choke as tears rush my eyes.

Rough hands on my body. Hands squeezing my breasts as I cry out uselessly.

You'll take what I give you, you worthless whore. The memory and the present mingle interchangeably. *And you'll love it so much you come the more I hurt you. You'll beg me to hurt you even more.*

"Oh yeah, you're a hot little bitch, aren't you?" The man behind me breathes into my face, slobbering and then biting painfully at my ear. "You hot for me, whore?"

I shudder at the words as it all washes over me. Knowing the pain is coming. The humiliation. The helplessness.

Worthless whore. You want it over? Then beg for it. Beg for it, whore!

It starts to rise, just like it always did and I hate myself. I hate him for making me this way. I hate him and I—

"Get the fuck away from her!"

My eyes pop open wide as I wrench my head to the right.

Just in time to see Dylan Lennox barreling towards us.

Oh shit.

CHAPTER THREE

DYLAN

I'll kill the fucker. It's the only thought I have as I tear into the guy and yank him off her. He goes down with little fight, throwing his arms over his face.

Miranda screams but all I can care about is the fact that I got him off her before he could. Before he could—

I roar in fury and bring my fist down on the fucker's face.

Once, then again, and—

I lift my fist to ram into his face again but arms wrap around me from behind. I look back in confusion.

It's Miranda. Dark mascara tear tracks line her cheeks from and she's shaking her head. "Stop. It's not what you think. Stop!"

What the fuck is she—

"He wasn't— He wasn't— I *wanted* it. We arranged this. Online. I knew he was going to be here."

She *wanted*—

I jerk back from both her and the guy I'm on top of. She tumbles backwards and the guy underneath me crawls away, dropping the condom he had clutched in his hand as he goes.

"You crazy fucks," he mutters as he crawls to his feet and limps away, hand to his bleeding face.

"You arranged for this." My voice is dead cold and my hands clench into fists. I still have the other fucker's blood on me. I'm sure I broke his nose.

Miranda just nods, her head down, sitting on the ground where she landed after I brushed her off me.

"You arrange for strangers to fucking rape you?"

Her head shoots up at this. "No! It's not... *that*. Not if I want it. We're consenting adults."

"Consenting—" I scoff, shaking my head. I can't fucking believe her. I drag my hands through my hair and turn away from her.

I rode the elevator up and then stood on the other side of the door for several long moments, warring with myself over whether or not to open it onto the roof. Just to peek. Just to double check she was fine getting to her car.

And when I lost the battle with myself and pushed open the door, only to find her struggling against that bastard and trying to scream...

"What the fuck is wrong with you?" I roar at her where she's still on the ground, dress up around her waist.

Jesus Christ, she's just exposed to the fucking world, not even trying to cover herself as she wipes at her eyes, only smearing the mascara worse.

I shouldn't have looked.

Fuck but I shouldn't have looked.

Because the sight of her there. Weeping. Broken. Legs splayed with one of her high heels broken, cunt bared...

It flips the switch I've managed for years to stifle. All the years of therapy, all the iron discipline.

Gone.

In a single moment, all of it, *gone*.

"Is this what you want?" I sneer, reaching down and grabbing her roughly by her upper arms, dragging her to her feet and then twirling her and slamming her face down on the hood of her Corvette.

I take both of her wrists and pin them behind her back. Then I bend over her from behind, just like that other bastard had her, and I jam my erection into her ass. "You want it like this? You want a stranger to fuck you?"

There's a distant voice shouting in the back of my head: *What the fuck are you doing? Let her go. Back away. Fucking* now. *This is a road you can never go down again.*

But then she bends her head to look at me, an awkward angle with the way I have her positioned. I can't read what's in her eyes. If it's lust or determination or what.

All I know is she doesn't look broken anymore.

"Yes, I want it," she whispers. "But only if you make it hurt."

My hand that's not holding her wrist is on my buckle the next instant. I rip it open and undo my slacks.

Fuuuuuuuuuuck, it feels good to free my cock. My tip immediately seeks her entrance. She's so hot. And wet. Dripping fucking wet.

She wants it.

And I haven't had it in so long. So fucking long.

Just this once. Just this once and then never again.

She *wants* it. It's not wrong if she wants it.

My hips surge forward and then I'm fucking her. It's not a decision. In this moment, I can't *not* be fucking her.

She cries out with the first in stroke. I don't ease her into it. And I'm a big motherfucker. Women have had trouble taking me in the past.

I pull back and then drive my hips forward again. Deeper. Fuck. I throw my head back and grip her wrists even tighter.

I'm not wearing a condom. Shit. It should worry me. But after six years without a woman, the only thing I can think is *fuck*, I can feel all of her. No barriers. Nothing between us. My nerve endings feel raw as if they're firing for the first time and the need to fuck her is this insane compulsion.

She clenches around me. Or maybe she's squeezing so tight because she's trying to keep me out? Is she regretting her decision?

The thought only makes me harder.

I put my hand on the back of her neck and shove her face harder into the hood of the car and I let my fantasies loose.

I followed her out of the bar. She was swinging that luscious ass so temptingly. Teasing all those bastards but then leaving them wanting.

Cock tease. My father's voice reverberates in my head. *Women who are cock teases need to be taught a lesson, son. A tease is a promise. It's our job to make sure they pay up.*

NO. I swore. I *swore* I'd never be anything like him.

Disgust chokes me.

But I fuck Miranda even harder. My hand pushes the side of her face against the hood. Fresh tears squeeze out of her eyes.

I'm horrified.

I'm fascinated.

She squeezes around me, tighter than my fist when I punish-fuck my hand for my sick fucking fantasies.

And I cum.

Deep and long and hard, I empty myself into her.

She squeezes tighter, tighter, milking me of every last drop, a high-pitched gasping wail escaping out her lips.

Fuck but she's cumming, too.

She really did want it.

I drag my cock out and then shove back in, rougher than I have yet, positively jackhammering into her and shoving her pelvis painfully against the hood of the Corvette.

So good. It's so good. So fuckin' good and I haven't had it in so long. My fantasies can't even compare—

Her nails scrabble against my arm where I hold her wrists and she shuts her eyes, pressing her forehead into the hood as her ass jerks and grinds against me. More pleased whines escape her mouth. Jesus Christ, is she *still* cumming?

My cock jerks inside her, still hard even after I've cum.

She's fucking magnificent.

She frowns and I can see she's finally coming down and I shake my head because fuck that.

My cock still impaling her, I drop her wrists and reach around to her clit. I pinch it cruelly at the same time I spit on my forefinger.

I reach down and then ruthlessly shove it up her ass.

Her eyes shoot open and her mouth drops into a wide O. But a second later her face is transformed again as she's lost in another wave of pleasure.

Oh fuck. Oh fuck yeah, that's right.

I pinch harder and shove another finger up her ass. I'm not gentle about it, either.

"You like that," I growl. I drag my hips back and forth slowly, my cock still stiff in her cunt. "You like it when I fucking defile you."

I shove a third finger in her ass. Fucking invading her. A stranger finger fucking her ass, almost dry. It's gotta hurt. It's gotta hurt a lot.

When I look at her face, I'm not disappointed. There are more tears. Pain amidst her pleasured whimpers.

She's hurting. You're hurting her.

The horror hits. What the fuck am I doing?

But then her back arches. She thrashes against the car hood and it's not in pain. Or maybe it is, partially. But by the look on her face, it's more pleasure than pain.

I shove my fingers ruthlessly farther up her ass. Pull them out. Shove them back up again even harder.

Her forehead scrunches with the pain. But she thrusts her ass back against my hand.

And I start fucking her again. With both my cock and my fingers.

Mercilessly.

Pulling out.

Then hammering back in.

Out.

Jackknifing in again.

The car bounces on its shocks with my every thrust and Miranda lets out small grunts each time.

I pull my fingers out of her ass and move my hand up her body.

To her throat.

I curve my hand around her neck, thumb at her pulse point. Her heartbeat is thrumming like a frightened rabbit's as I continue to fuck her.

I fuck her and fuck her and fuck her.

How long has it been since I last came? Five minutes? Ten?

I squeeze my fingers around her throat and her breath hitches. I test the pressure and her rasping gasp makes pleasure spike down my spine.

She can still breathe, but barely.

I lean over her back and growl in her ear. "I could end it so easily. If I squeezed just a little harder. Is this how you like to play? You want the pain? You like the fucking danger of meeting strangers on rooftops where no one will hear you scream?"

She nods into my grip.

Fucking *nods*.

It infuriates me so much that I lose my fucking mind and squeeze harder for a couple of seconds just to teach her a damn lesson.

She needs to be scared fucking straight.

Almost the second my grip tightens, though, she comes. Fucking *comes*. Again.

"You stupid fucking idiot," I hiss in her ear, loosening my grip on her throat and moving my hand to cover her mouth.

I'm disgusted with myself the second I do it. But it also feels so fucking *right*. She can't scream now. I grip my hand over her mouth even harder, pulling her head back against my chest as I ram my dick into her cunt.

My fingers offer just enough clearance of her nose so she can breathe. The thought is a distant comfort.

It doesn't change the brutal scene.

Or how much I'm fucking getting off on it.

Because being back inside a slick cunt, having my hands on a woman again, like *this*, after so long, so many *years* without—Jesus Christ.

Her silky, dark hair is up in an elegant updo and I lean down and bite the back of her neck, roaring as I come again. Harder than the first time. So much harder.

My teeth sink into her sweet, soft flesh as the last of my cum pumps into her cunt that's squeezed like a vice around my cock.

She cries out against my hand and I roar into the nape of her neck in animal satisfaction.

And then—

Then...

I'm left heaving over her back, my mouth slack against her neck.

I blink and it's like coming back from a bout of insanity.

I pull my hand away from her mouth and jerk away from her, my cock finally slipping out of her.

I stumble backwards and my mouth drops open in horror at the scene before me.

Miranda is splayed face down on the hood of her car, legs awkwardly spread as cum drips down her leg and fuck—

I can see the bite mark on the back of her neck from five feet away. Did I draw blood?

She's blinking too and turning to look at me. Her face is a mess of mascara and tears. She looks fucking battered and broken.

By me.

Another voice rings out in my head. Not my father this time, but another monster even more insidious. *If you do it right, you can break them and they'll still beg you for more. That's when you'll know you're a god.*

"I'm sorry," I rasp, roughly jerking my pants up and shoving my dick back inside. "I'm so sorry."

She starts to shake her head but I hold up my hands and then I turn and fucking sprint toward the door.

CHAPTER FOUR

MIRANDA

I'm still shaken the next morning as I sit in my office and check my lipstick in the small compact I keep in my desk. Cherry ripe red. My signature color. At least it has been for the last few years.

Back in college, I wore a shade called Pale Iris. It might as well have been called Insignificant Iris. Invisible Iris.

I wanted so badly to stand out back then. To be somebody. And when, right out of college, the budding mega-star in the business world, Bryce Gentry took notice of me, meager Miranda, minor Miranda, miniscule Miranda, it felt like the light of the universe was finally shining on me.

Like maybe finally, after a lifetime on the sidelines, I could be the star of someone's show. Maybe even my own.

And look how well that went. Maybe that was what you got when you relied on someone else to find you.

I got swallowed up in him instead.

And he was the worst kind of man, the kind who will devour you whole instead of giving you the strength to stand on your own two feet beside him.

And Dylan?

What kind of man is he?

I check the rest of my face in the small mirror. I was in a rush this morning because I overslept my alarm after tossing and turning all night. After two back to back meetings, it's the first time all morning I've had a second to myself.

In the mirror, my blue eyes look too large and cartoonish in my face. At least the circles under them from my restless night are only slightly visible after working my magic with concealer.

I snap the compact shut and run my hand from my temple down to my throat, brushing my fingers across the skin where Dylan's hand gripped me so roughly last night.

I once read an article that said you can tell everything about a man by the way he fucks. And I wonder if, after last night, maybe it's true.

I shudder again as I close my eyes and relive every moment. I bite my lip as I recall the feel of his huge cock breeching me. The merciless way he thrust into me.

But then his hand was on my clit, making sure I was right there with him. Occasionally I felt him pause like he was checking in on me before continuing.

Or is that just wishful thinking?

After all, how many years have I been searching for the perfect man? Someone who will be a bastard to me in the bedroom—or on the hood of my car—but could be a gentleman the rest of the time?

Of course I don't know if Dylan Lennox is a gentleman the rest of the time. But I've read up on him. He and his brother Darren are the entrepreneurial duo who came on the robotics scene six years ago with a vengeance, taking up an impressive market share almost from the get-go.

Dylan's never seen with women in public. Some speculate it's because he's still in the closet but I know the real reason.

It's because of Bryce Gentry.

The mutual skeleton in both our closets.

When Bryce finally went to jail for his crimes two years ago after the man he was blackmailing, Jackson Vale, caught him trying to commit corporate espionage, all the dirt Bryce had on Jackson and everyone else in his blackmail files went public.

Including a story on Dylan Lennox that was a small blip in the flood of the Gentry Files, as they came to be known. A story about Dylan brutalizing a prostitute.

It was there and then gone the next day. Disappeared.

I made it my personal mission to follow every story that Jackson released. Because though the story might have disappeared, Jackson was my ex and we were still friendly. I contacted him and he gave me a copy of the files directly.

There were pictures of Dylan and the prostitute. Him holding her down, hands around her throat. Her crying and trying to shove him away from her. They were the kind of pictures that would have made any other woman shrink away and avoid Dylan completely.

But both Jackson and I were willing to suspend judgement a little longer. We both know that Bryce liked to create circumstances and then take pictures as 'proof' of a salacious story, or even a crime, to get dirt on a competitor or enemy. Then use it as leverage against them to blackmail them, whether or not it was true.

I now know it's how Bryce's company Gentry Tech rose in prestige so quickly. Every permit he needed, he was granted. Funding he requested magically went through. Contracts were won amid stiff and more experienced competition. He got patents before anyone else.

But it was a house of cards that Jackson brought tumbling down. Bryce bribed judges, government officials, contractors, employees from other companies to get confidential product information to reverse engineer and delay their patents so Bryce could get the patents first.

Bryce tried to take as many people down with him as he could. Hence the story on Dylan. But why had it disappeared so quickly? Jackson didn't know why.

So I tracked down the prostitute, Lenore Richards—who was no longer a prostitute, but living in a two bedroom in south San Jose with her two children—and asked her.

And got a door slammed in my face.

But I persisted. At the time, I wasn't even sure why. I just had to know. What kind of man was Dylan Lennox?

Was he the kind of man who hurt women against their will?

... or with their *permission*?

It's a difference that wouldn't matter to a lot of women. But to me? To me it meant everything.

So I staked out her house like a crazy person. Every time she left, at least when she wasn't with her children, I followed her to her car, peppering her with questions.

"Look, lady, I could call the cops on you," she exploded on the second day. "I got rights. Reporters can't just be showing up at my house—"

"I'm not a reporter! I told you I'm not. I just need to know. Did Dylan rape you that night? Please. I'm only asking for myself. As a woman."

Lenore breathed out and looked around us. She lived in the bottom level of a townhouse and the small cul-de-sac was quiet.

"Look, I don't want no trouble. I ain't said nothing to nobody just like I promised in the paperwork."

Paperwork. So she *was* paid to stay quiet. Did that mean Dylan was guilty of what they said he was?

I held up my hands. "I won't make trouble. I just need to know. For myself."

She frowned. "You know him or somethin'?"

I nodded even though it wasn't exactly true. "We've run into each other here and there."

She hefted out a long breath. "Naw, he didn't rape me. Paid me extra for all that kinky shit is all. But you didn't hear nothing from me."

Then she backed away from me. "You leavin' now?"

"But if he didn't.... then why didn't you just say so? Why would he pay for you not to clear his name?"

"You said you'd go if I answered your question."

She looked pissed so I backed up just like she did, nodding vigorously. "You'll never see me again."

She narrowed her eyes at me but I was already halfway back to my car. I had what I'd come for.

Regardless of the reason for the payoff, I believed her. Dylan Lennox wasn't a rapist.

But he did like the game.

Just like me.

I check my reflection one last time in the mirror, flashing a smile.

Packaged perfection.

My smile drops. Outwardly perfect, anyway. I can only keep up the illusion for so long. And being this person, the Miranda in the Mirror, means I can never be truly intimate with anyone.

I just want someone I don't have to pretend with.

So no matter how much last night might have scared him or freaked him out, I've been excited by the possibility of him for far too long to let this go without another try.

I look at my calendar for the day.

Yep, I can afford to take an early lunch.

I'm just pulling my purse out from under my desk when there's a knock on my door. Then Chet pushes the door open without waiting for my reply, naturally.

"Miranda," he says, his smile wide, bright white teeth flashing. "You look lovely today."

"I'm just on my way out, Chet. What is it?" I swing my purse over my shoulder to illustrate my point.

Chet steps further into the room and lets the door shut behind him. "Can't I stop in to see how you're doing?"

I sigh, looking down at my phone.

"Chet, we aren't dating anymore. If you have something to say about something work related, you don't have to come by, you can just—"

"I just don't understand it, Rany," he says, coming in and sitting down in one of the chairs in front of my desk. Ugh, I always hated that nickname. "We were so good together. Everyone looked at us and thought we were that perfect *it couple*. We had the kind of relationship everyone dreams of having."

I can only stare at him, my mouth slightly ajar. Is that what he really thought?

Fine. Apparently we're having this conversation here and now. I broke up with him two weeks ago and he's been calling and texting every day since. At least I assume he continued to. I blocked his number on day four because I didn't want to deal with it anymore.

I sigh and look at him now. "Didn't you think it was strange how I always wore my makeup all the time when we were together? Or odd that I never wanted you to sleep over?"

Chet frowns. "I guess. But girls get weird about how they look or whatever. And you have insomnia and can't sleep with someone else in your bed. I respected that. And I lov—"

"No, Chet, you don't." I shake my head. "I was never myself when I was with you, don't you get it? You don't even *know* the real me."

No one does. Because I don't let them in. I'm so careful with the Miranda in the Mirror. Maybe Chet fell in love with her. But she's a fantasy.

"I was tired of pretending," I say, coming around the desk. For a while, when I first started dating Chet six months ago, I thought that maybe, if I tried hard enough, just *maybe*, I *could* be her. That pretty, normal woman. Maybe if I worked hard enough, I could get it to stick. If I had the right man, the right job, the right clothes...

But then we'd have sex, and no matter how Chet tried, he couldn't make me cum. He was too much of a gentleman in bed. Or, more likely, too much of a wimp. I asked him to spank me a couple of times and he half-heartedly smacked my bottom. Eventually I gave up and just pretended to cum every time because it was easier and made Chet happy.

I ended it after I woke up in a cold sweat after another nightmare. I was back in Bryce's apartment and he was humiliating me and hurting me. I woke up sobbing. And then I touched myself and came almost immediately after a months-long dry spell.

I broke up with Chet the next day and went to see that woman Lenore the day after that.

"I'm sorry. I wasn't fair to you and I'm sorry."

Chet stands and walks to the door, not looking at me. He's hurt and obviously trying to hide it. "Rod wanted me to ask you if you made any headway with Lennox last night."

"What?" I ask, too sharply. What do they know about what happened with me and Dylan last night?

Chet looks my way, frowning at my overreaction.

"He asked you to talk to him at the conference, right? To see if he'd give up any information on if they were considering ProDynamics' bid? On our processors?"

"Oh, right." My heartbeat slows a bit. "No. I didn't get a chance to talk to him." It was true. We hadn't done much talking. Our encounter had been more of a... physical nature.

"Dammit, you know we need that contract, Miranda. Why didn't you try harder? God knows you don't have a problem using your... attributes," he looks right at my chest, "when you really want something."

And here's the other reason why I broke up with Chet. Because sometimes he can be a misogynistic asshole, which, if I'm honest, was part of my attraction to him. Cause I'm fucked up like that. He just couldn't keep it up in bed, which is the only place I really need or want it.

"Don't let the door hit your ass on the way out, Chet. I'm taking an early lunch." I brush past him.

"Hi there, is Dylan Lennox in?"

"You have an appointment?" A shrewd woman in her mid-fifties looks over her spectacles at me in the lobby of Lennox Brothers Corp.

"Just tell him Miranda Rose has stopped in to see him."

Her eyes narrow in scrutiny. "Mr. Lennox is a busy man."

I get what she's not saying. He doesn't have time to pause his important work for every hussy that stops in wanting to chat with one of the industry's most eligible bachelors.

I smile, humoring her. "I think he might want to see me."

Of course, he could very well order his assistant here to send me away without ever uttering a word to me in person.

Somehow I have a feeling he's classier than that. Then again, that might just be the man I've built him up to be in my mind as I've obsessed over him the past six months. But isn't that why I'm here? To try to separate fact from fiction and let go of this fascination once and for all?

Still frowning at me, the assistant ushers me to sit in one of the lobby chairs while she picks up her phone and murmurs into it.

Her eyes dart over to me and I see the surprise register there. I only barely suppress a grin. Aha, so Dylan's not the cowardly sort after all. He's going to see me.

The assistant clears her throat and then stands. "This way, Miss."

She leads me to the door to the left of her desk, pushes through it, and then heads down a long hallway. It soon opens up to a large warehouse like space.

There are a couple of rows of cubicles but they're interspersed with portions of the room where various robotics components are set up. Some are in pieces, but there are several large robotic arms taller than a car that whir and twist as technicians poke and prod at them.

It all looks a little like the time I went to NASA when I was visiting my cousin in Houston that one time.

We go down the wall of the room and to the back of the building. There the matronly assistant knocks on the door.

"Come in," comes Dylan's low, manly voice. Even the sound of it sends shivers down my body.

I reach for the door handle but the assistant gets there ahead of me and opens the door.

Dylan's sitting behind his desk, intimidating and hulking as he stares darkly past his secretary at me.

"Thank you, Hannah," he says, eyes still on me. "You may go."

"Do you need water or tea, sir?"

He gives a hard shake of his head. "No, that will be all. Hold all my calls."

Hannah flashes me a distrustful glance and then backs out of the room, shutting the door as she goes.

Dylan's nostrils flare as soon as the door shuts. "What are you doing here?"

I bristle a little at his bark, but only a little. I've been a sub to dominant men before and I know my coming here breaks all sorts of rules.

But Dylan's not a dominant, at least not in the traditional or contractual sense. And maybe I could play it coy and wait a week before contacting him but I don't do that. I don't do games.

So I stride forward and sit in the chair opposite his desk and pull it closer, then lean in. "Look, last night was..."

Shit. I had a whole speech prepared but it suddenly completely leaves my head as his dark eyes pierce mine.

Looking into them last night for the first time had a similar effect but it was more manageable because of the dimness of the ballroom and darkness of the roof. But here, in the light of day...

"Last night was regrettable," he snaps, finishing my sentence. I immediately start shaking my head but he's on a roll now. "Last night was something that will never, and I mean, *never*, be repeated."

I feel my cheeks heat at this, and not in embarrassment. I haven't even been here all of five minutes and here he is, already pissing me off.

"Do you know how long I've looked for someone like you? Someone real? You think I like setting up half-satisfying fucks online?"

He shoots up from his chair and bangs both fists down on his desk. "That's fucking irresponsible and you'll never do it again. Jesus, we didn't even use a goddamned condom!"

"I always use a condom. It was just with you that I—" I stop when I can see he doesn't believe me, then press on anyway, no matter how angry I'm getting. "And I have an IUD, so don't worry."

He just shakes his head.

"That doesn't change anything. You could get seriously hurt. You don't know who the hell will show up."

My eyebrows shoot to my hairline. "Oh yeah? What the hell else am I supposed to do?"

"Try controlling your urges. Discipline. Ever heard of it?"

I laugh at that. "Because you were so disciplined as you fucked me against the hood of my car last night. Twice."

He sucks in a huge breath and then releases it, looking like he's about to start breathing fire. Shit. This isn't how I meant for this to go.

I didn't come in here to antagonize him. It's not going to get either of us what we want.

I just wanted to make my proposal, tempt him with my sexy top and cleavage, and get out leaving him wanting more. Okay so shit, maybe I *do* like playing games a little. But only because I know this could be good for both of us. With how ravenously he took me, I know he wants this, too.

"Look," I say, trying to pacify him and salvage the situation. "Everybody has needs. They're nothing to be ashamed of. If we can find a safe, mutually beneficial way to meet those needs, what's the harm?"

He shakes his head and speaks through his teeth. "Some desires are shameful."

I stand up from my chair and take a step back at that. I can't help it. It stings. He thinks I should be asham—

"Fuck. I didn't mean *you*. It's fine for you to want whatever you— But for me, it's not, I can't *ever*—" He rakes a hand through his hair just like he did last night, looking flustered and pained at the same time. It looks like a deep pain, too.

He closes his eyes and breathes out before piercing me again with that gaze.

"This will never happen, Miss Rose. I'm not the man to scratch your itch. Find someone else. Please leave now."

But I didn't get where I am today by being meek. I didn't survive Bryce Gentry by walking gently into that good night. No, sir.

I'm stubborn. There were nights, more than one, where I felt so worthless I wanted to give up and die.

But I didn't. I'm here today and everything I've gotten after Bryce was because I stubbornly stood up, demanded, and took it.

"I'll leave on one condition."

Dylan looks exasperated and throws his hands out.

"Give me your phone number and I'll leave right this minute."

"What? Is this some sort of fucking game to you?"

I'm the one breathing out hard this time. Shit. Games again. "Maybe. I don't know. I try to be as straightforward as I can. I'm not trying to fuck with your life."

He scoffs. "Aren't you?"

"We're both single. And unless you're celibate, you need, how did you put it, you need to get your itches scratched too. Why not with me? Someone you can trust to be discrete. I'll sign an NDA or anything else if you're worried about that, show you my test results, I know we didn't use protection the other night but I'm clean and on the pill and I—"

"Jesus Christ, you say giving you my phone number will shut you up and get you out of my office the quickest?" He yanks open the top drawer on his desk and shoves his phone my way. "Have at it."

I stare at the phone but only for a second before snatching it up and punching my number in. I hit the green dial button and wait for my phone in my purse to buzz before hanging up.

I know I'm being pushy as hell, unattractively so. Maybe this all goes nowhere. Probably this all goes nowhere. Probably he blocks my number the second I walk out his office door.

Still I add myself to his contacts and hope for the best. Stranger things have happened. And when I glance back up at him, it's to find him quickly averting his eyes.

He was watching me.

He's attracted to me.

He followed me to that garage roof last night. He's intrigued. Maybe my pushiness today killed any interest.

Or maybe he remembers exactly why he hung around last night after he came the first time and kept on fucking me for another half hour. Maybe he remembers exactly how incredible it felt for both of us to give into the animal and let ourselves *free*. For once, finally *free*.

I incline my head as I lean over to place his phone back on his desk. Does it afford a spectacular view of my cleavage? Yes, yes it does, and yes, I hope he's looking.

"My ass is still sore from your fingers last night," I whisper.

And then I turn and head out the door.

CHAPTER FIVE

DYLAN

My ass is still sore... said with that impish little saucy grin.

I shake my head at her audacity for what feels like the hundredth time.

"I told Hannah never to let her back to my office if she comes again." I stride back and forth on the well-worn path in Dr. Laghari's office.

"I don't need this shit. I've been doing so well in my recovery and then to fuck it up so bad like I did last night." I shake my head again. "Fucking maddening."

Dr. Laghari doesn't say anything for a long moment so I look over at him.

"What, you think last night wasn't fucking up my sexual sobriety?"

He inclines his head. "I've never used that term. You came up with it yourself. But it's interesting that you see having sex for the first time in four years in terms of an addict going back to a drug."

"Isn't it?" I throw my hands up. Fuck, I know I'm being dramatic, but I could use with the good doctor being a little more... well, a little *more*. I expected him to look, I don't know, disappointed when I came in today and told him about last night. But the last half hour all he's done is ask me how I *felt* about what happened.

I *feel* like I want to crawl out of my own fucking skin, that's how I feel. I never wanted to be in that position ever again, standing over a weeping girl after putting my hands on her.

But there I was, having come fucking *twice*. And even then, at the end when I was horrified looking down at her so broken, still there was a part of me that *loved* it. That loved seeing her there like that, that loved knowing it was me who'd done it to her. That wanted to grab her by her silky brunette hair, shove her face down and immediately do it to her all over again.

"We talked about you eventually dating again and what it might be like to sleep with a woman after your years of self-imposed celibacy. Wasn't this what all our time together has been working toward?"

"Me dating was always a hypothetical," I say. "And Jesus, no, all this therapy has been to try to keep these fucked up desires from *ever* coming out again. It's been about learning discipline to keep myself in fucking check. So I don't hurt people. Hurt *women*."

"Like your father did."

"Yes, like my father did."

"Do you think what you did last night and what your father did to your mother all those years are the same?"

"Yes!" I explode. I stomp back toward the window and drop my hands to the small ledge, staring out at the city. "No. I don't fucking know."

I squeeze my eyes shut and image after image flashes through my head. There was the time Dad shoved Mom against the kitchen counter and bent her over until her face was buried in the burned casserole until she couldn't breathe, arms flailing.

Or when he grabbed her by the neck and forced her upstairs. When she tripped near the top, he got so mad, he threw her back down them. She rolled and screamed as she fell down half the staircase before catching hold of the banister. He yelled at her for being a dumb, clumsy slut. Not checking to see if she was okay, he just yanked up her skirt right there on the staircase and…

I open my eyes and look out the window like the sky can banish the memories that form the fundamental core of who I am.

I kept my little brother Darren from seeing the worst of it. He's a kinky bastard but he never pushes it near the line. We've shared women a time or two in the past and he doesn't have the same sick urges I do. He's the fun one, always the life of the party.

Darren, yes, Darren, I protected from Dad.

But Chloe, just a year younger than Dare? Jesus Christ, little Chloe...

I swallow and my eyes fall shut again.

"Even if it's not the exact same as what my dad did to my mom, it's still too fucked up. To get off on that... when I know what it— what it can do..." I shake my head and swipe my forearm roughly against the tears stinging at my eyes.

"It sounds like last night brought up a lot of the things you've been trying to push down and ignore for a long time," says Dr. Laghari. "And that's okay if that's how you needed to deal with what happened. But at least consider that this might be an opportunity to reconsider how you approach dealing with the trauma you went through."

"Trauma *I* went through—?" I turn back to the doctor. He's got to be kidding.

"Have you thought any more about trying to contact your sister?"

Jesus, doc, way to kick a guy when he's down. "She wouldn't want to hear from me."

"How do you know if you don't try?"

I scoff and shake my head. "I'm pretty fucking sure. I let her down her entire life. Besides, if she wanted to talk to me, she has my number."

Dr. Laghari just shrugs. "Maybe she thinks the same about you. If he wanted to talk to me, he has my number."

Jesus Christ, why do I even come here? I rake my hands through my hair. Okay, so after all the shit hit the fan, Dr. Laghari helped me through the worst of it. There was awhile there when I didn't think I deserved to live. It was only doc and knowing my brother needed me that kept me from swallowing the bottle of pills on my nightstand.

Darren had lost everyone, and he didn't even know why. I couldn't just cut out on him, too.

But how the fuck was I supposed to live with the knowledge that my father was the worst kind of monster and I was just like him?

I thought discipline was the answer. I'd just never give in to those desires. Ever again.

But now doc is saying that, what? That that kind of discipline is impossible? That he always knew I'd fail and be back here, fighting this shit?

"I swore I'd never be like him." My voice is so low and guttural I barely recognize it. "I'll die before ever becoming anything like that fucking bastard."

"Dylan." Dr. Laghari calls my name but I don't look at him. "*Dylan.*"

A few seconds later, he moves into my field of vision. Damn, I actually made him get up off that chair he always sits in. This really must be a crisis.

"Dylan," he says again, his lined face gentle with compassion. "You grew up in a violent household. You witnessed horrific things, not just once, but over and over again. The women you loved, your mother and sister, were hurt by a man you loved, your father."

I want to deny it. I want to say that he's wrong and that I hated my father. But I didn't, at least not growing up. I think I do now. I think the hate has choked out all the love. Because how could I love a man who did the things he did…?

"It's not wrong for you to have grown up being confused about sex. The way your sexual education developed may have been unhealthy, or fucked up, as you say. The things that happened in that house were seriously fucked up."

Hearing the words *fucked up* come out of Dr. Laghari's clipped and slightly accented voice sounds wrong and oddly hilarious.

But I don't laugh, if only because in all the years I've been coming to him, the doc has never gotten up and spoken to me so frankly. It feels like it goes against some shrink code and I go still.

"But none of that means you're doomed to be just like your father. The kinks you like as far as your sexual appetite don't mean you want to hurt or control women the way he did. We've talked extensively about how abuse is about control much more than sexual gratification. From everything you've told me, that sort of control and abuse is abhorrent to you. Inflicting pain without consent is one of your greatest fears. It's all but a primal fear for you, you hate it so much."

"But what if..." I trail off. Dr. Laghari is being so frank with me, fuck, it breaks something down and I finally ask the question that truly terrifies me. "But what if I secretly want it?" And after that all the other questions come pouring out. "What if I *want* to hurt them without their consent? What if I give in to it and find I like it too much? And I become a monster just like him?"

I expect Dr. Laghari to pull back. At the very least, I expect his features to became wary at this admission of my deepest fears. Because he'll finally see me for what I am:

A monster lurking in a man's skin.

But instead he laughs and shakes his head, clapping me on the back.

Fucking *laughs*.

"What the fuck, doc?" I jerk back from him.

But he's still just shaking his head, a fond smile on his face. "Oh Dylan, Dylan. Shh, I will tell you something, but it'll just be between us, all right?"

I nod, feeling bewildered.

He leans in and raises his hand to his mouth like he's really going to tell me a secret. "You are not a sociopath. I'm old and I've met a few in my time. You aren't one. You have the capacity to empathize with others. You worry about whether you're hurting the people around you. By definition, that means you aren't a sociopath."

"You'll be just fine." He claps me on the back again. "See you next week, my friend. See you next week."

I stumble out of his office, half confused, half more relieved than I've ever felt in my life. Is it really that easy? I just needed someone, a professional who knows what he's talking about, to tell me I'm not a sociopath? And pow, I'm cured?

I'm still frowning as I walk toward my car but I have to admit, I do feel a fuck of a lot lighter than when I walked in.

Is it possible that I'm just... *me*? That I'm not my father's creation, doomed from my very DNA? But if I thought that, then I'd have to believe the same of Darren, wouldn't I? And he came out okay. Better than okay.

Jesus, I don't know a more carefree person than my little brother. I love that damn kid. He's not a kid anymore but to me, he'll always be my little brother. I kept him from the worst of it, and that last, terrible revelation— I shudder. He'll never know, not if I can keep it from him.

Both Dad and Mom are gone. Maybe the past really *can* finally be buried.

Easy for you to say. What about Chloe?

I pull out my phone and click 'Contacts'. There's Chloe's number, just where it's been all these years. Transferred from phone to phone as I upgraded over the years. Never dialed.

My thumb hovers over the *call* button.

When suddenly the phone buzzes with an incoming text message.

Saved by the text. I breathe out and switch over to look at the text.

It's from Miranda.

There are three addresses with a short note under each.

The first says: *Any night this week after 8pm except Fri. Key under the doormat*.

The second reads: *Tomorrow, 6-8. My car will be 'stalled' on the side of the road*.

And the third: *Friday. 11pm. Back alley behind Club Chandelier*.

Followed by: *My safe word is red*.

My blood immediately fires red hot. My cock goes stiff and I'm completely fucking pissed. Is this what she would do with those fucking guys off the internet? Give them locations to 'attack' her? Did she let *them* know where the fucking key to her *house* is?

Jesus fucking Christ.

Somebody needs to teach this woman a fucking lesson on safety. I hiss out a long breath at the possibilities that immediately begin flashing through my mind. Followed by the revulsion that's a knee jerk reaction.

You are not a sociopath.

Before I fully admit what I'm doing, I'm in my car, punching her address into my GPS.

CHAPTER SIX

MIRANDA

I was distracted for the rest of the day and barely got anything done after going to Dylan's office at lunch. I think I answered some emails. Then daydreamed about Dylan. Maybe scheduled a few meetings? Daydreamed about Dylan some more.

I cancelled happy hour plans with Daniel and came home early. After today, I just wanted a glass of wine and a *long* bath. But Daniel is my bff and I know I'm gonna hear an earful about it on Friday when we're planning to hang out again.

He's having drama with his new Domme, shocking, and I know he wanted to tell me all about it. Frankly, the fact that he's been in a semi-stable relationship for as long as he has—a whole three months—is one of the things that gives me hope for myself.

Maybe not with Dylan. He never responded to my texts. Though I guess that's part of the point of those kinds of texts. I just put them out there and not knowing whether the guy will pick up the ball or not is part of the thrill of it.

With guys online we usually play over video chat a few times and then I meet them at the The Dungeon, my favorite local BDSM club, at least once before I send out the kind of open invitation I just sent Dylan. And I've never invited anyone to play at my actual *house* before.

But I'm breaking all the rules with Dylan. Which I guess is part of the point. I don't want rules. I want to be free. Free to be as fucked up as I can be with someone who knows the score.

Outside The Dungeon. Outside sane. Outside safe.

All I need is consensual.

Is that fucked up?

I never pretended to be anything else.

I open the fridge and bend over to reach for the leftover fried rice from yesterday. Maybe if I—

I screech as I'm suddenly grabbed from behind.

A huge hand clamps over my mouth and an arm tightens like a steel band around my waist, pulling me into a body. A large, male body. A large, *aroused* male body.

What if it's not Dylan?

Leaving the key under the mat is stupid. Really stupid. Everyone puts their spare key there.

It could be anyone behind me. It's dark out and I always leave my shutters open because I secretly like the thought of someone watching me. Looking in when I can't see out.

What if someone's been watching me?

What if someone saw me put the key under the mat?

"Don't say a word, bitch," comes the growl in my ear. Low. Gutteral.

I can't tell if it's Dylan or not.

The hand not at my mouth grabs at my breast with a bruising grip and I cry out.

"What?" he sneers. "You aren't even going to fight me?"

What if it's not Dylan? *What if it's not fucking Dylan?* Oh God. Oh God oh God oh God.

I start freaking the fuck out, fighting and screaming and biting to get away. The man behind me, oh shit, he only gets harder as he yanks me out of the kitchen and shoves me to the carpeted floor of the living room.

His cock digs into my ass.

I twist my head to get a look at him. I just need to know it's Dylan. I just need to know. Then everything will be okay.

But he's wearing a fucking ski mask.

He does let go of my mouth as he shoves me face first to the carpet, though. And when his big, brutal body leans over mine, I ask in a desperate whisper, "Dylan?"

There's a brief pause though his grip on my wrists he has wrenched behind my back is no gentler.

"You want to say a color, little girl?" he barks. But the growling rasp is gone from his voice and it's recognizable. It's Dylan. I bow my forehead to the carpet as my heartbeat slows. It's not real. It's Dylan.

It's Dylan and I could end all this with a single word. *Red*.

Instead, I arch my ass up and start to fight like a wildcat at the same time. I'm suddenly furious at him for scaring me. Furious at myself for my fuckedupness and how thrilled I am by the fear. Furious at everything.

"No, you fucking bastard," I spit. "I don't need to say a fucking color. I need you to get the fuck out of my house. You can't fucking have me."

I twist against his grip and his knee in my back even as I hear the noise of his zipper coming undone. My belly swoops at the sound as he laughs in my ear.

"You think you can get away from me?" The rasp is back in his voice. "You're all alone. Your neighbors are too far away to hear you even if you scream. You're at my mercy. I can do anything I want to you."

As if to punctuate his point, he reaches up under my skirt, wrenches my panties to the side, and shoves three fingers up inside me.

I can't help making an *oof* noise at the intrusion. I'm not wet yet and it stings. I scrabble at the carpet, trying to crawl away from him. It's no use, though.

He just grabs hold of my leg and drags me backwards toward him. I cry out, letting all of it go. Letting all of it fucking *go*.

Probably a really dumb move. I don't know Dylan. Not really. But still, just like last night, I give myself over to him in complete trust.

Which doesn't mean I submit. No, the struggle is part of what I love, what I need.

So I kick at him and scream. I must land one especially good kick because he grunts loudly and then launches himself at me as I make another attempt to get away.

He lands on top of me, his whole body covering all of mine.

His erection is bigger and harder than last time, though I wouldn't have thought that was possible. "You think you can fight me, slut?" He laughs humorlessly. "I'll show you what sluts like you deserve. To have their cunts full of cock."

And with that, I feel him bare against my ass. He reaches one hand around my hips, yanking me up just enough to expose my pussy.

And then he jams inside me.

We both cry out at his entrance and I squeeze around him. Because it feels.

So.

Damn.

Good.

He is everything I've been missing. That emptiness I've been walking around with years. For *years*. But now I'm full in every way.

He drags out and then shoves in again and I come.

Two thrusts and I come.

That's how badly I've needed this.

I scream into the carpet with my orgasm, thrashing on his cock. I hope he thinks its because I'm still trying to get away. He can't know how desperate I am for him. How goddamned needy.

I should know better, though.

"You think it's that easy? You think you get off that easy? You don't know how this works, little girl."

He bottoms out inside me, so deep it makes my breath catch. And then he pulls all the way out and flips me so that I'm on my back.

Immediately, though, he's back on top of me, grabbing my ankles and lifting them up so they're up near my head. He plunges in again relentlessly. One stroke, then two.

His cock is big, but for me, it's the perfect size. Wide enough to stretch me and provide sensation to every part of my sex, and long enough to hit all the important bits inside when he thrusts deep.

But when he withdraws and I feel the head of his cock nudging at my ass, my eyes fly wide open.

"No!" I shout, looking him in the eye.

His dark eyes are piercing as I frantically meet his gaze.

But then he just reaches down and continues feeding his cock into my asshole.

Will I let him do this? I haven't let other men. No one since...

I whimper but don't avert my gaze from Dylan's. Shit. Oh shit, oh shit, am I really letting him do this?

He's a thief. You don't have a choice.

But that's just the game. We both know that he's waiting to see if I'll say the safe word or not.

Isn't this what I wanted, though? Not to be in control? For a man to be able to take me to all the darkest, deepest places?

So I purse my lips tight, lay back, and close my eyes.

He doesn't wait. He immediately surges deeper.

Oh God! Ow, fuck. Ow! I cry out and my eyes fly open, because fuck, it *hurts*. He's going to split me wide open.

"Look at me," he barks. "Eyes on me or I'll fucking kill you."

I nod obediently, both thrilled and terrified at his words.

But his cock, oh *God*. It was the perfect size for my pussy, but my *ass*? It hurts. It hurts so bad.

Tears spring to my eyes but Dylan doesn't stop.

What he does do is yank the mask off his head and throw it to the side. Then he bends over, my legs sandwiched up between our bodies, crushing me to the carpet with his weight

"That's right," he whispers, rasp gone.

It's just the two of us in this moment. Dylan and Miranda.

"Let me see you cry. Show me how it hurts."

So I do.

I let it all go. I fucking sob as he continues breeching me, inch by terrible inch until he's finally buried in my ass.

He jams in the last bit and I cry harder. He smiles in satisfaction and leans over to kiss my face. Kissing my tears. Licking them.

"That's right. Cry for me, little girl."

He pulls out and then his hips thrust back in. I screech at the repeated invasion and he grips my hair at the nape of my neck, gathering it in his hand and jerking my head so that I can't avert my eyes.

"Fucking look at me while I defile you, angel."

So I do. Tears pouring down my cheeks, I look up at him and wonder who this cruel and terrible and fucked up and perfect man is.

Perfect for me.

I've had men who wanted to hurt me before. With whips and paddles and canes. But this is what I've needed. For the *sex itself* to hurt.

For my partner to *want* it to hurt.

And I see it so clearly in his eyes. He wants to punish me. He wants to fuck me until I sob. The satisfaction and intensity and pleasure burning in his eyes as he looks down on me, our faces so close we're sharing a breath—

A shudder wracks my body as I come again, harder than before.

I see his surprise as he feels it. His eyes widen in wonder.

And then his mouth comes crashing down on mine. His tongue is as invasive as his cock and I bite and suck on it as I continue coming, the wave hot and sharp and bright, fizzling out through my limbs as we continue to kiss and fuck.

It's only seconds later when I feel him stiffen and then his fingers clench my hair even tighter and he kisses me harder then ever as he pumps cum deep in my ass.

He rolls us to the side, cradling my head on his arm as we both gasp for breath in the moments afterwards.

Holy *shit*.

Did that really just—

I mean... holy *shit*.

That was the hottest and best sex of my life, bar none. And most of it was *anal*. What the hell? I hate anal. I've always hated anal. Haven't I?

I've only done it a few times before. All with Bryce and all when he was punishing me with some new mindfuck.

But this... this was something altogether different.

Dylan kisses the top of my head as he cradles me to his chest and I feel like bursting out in a fresh round of tears.

A few minutes later, he gets up and gently helps me to my feet. Without a word, he finds my bedroom with attached bathroom and starts a bath running. The water quickly steams the mirror and hairs on my arm prickle. I feel cold as my sweaty skin cools.

A minute later, Dylan takes my hand and together, we step into my large bathtub. It's one of the few luxuries my house affords. All property in the Bay Area is ridiculously expensive, but I chose this house in particular because, even though smaller in square footage overall, it has this extra-large bathroom, including the jacuzzi tub. I'm so busy at work I'm rarely home, but when I am, I like to enjoy the creature comforts.

Dylan fiddles with the settings on the jets. I'm about to offer to turn them on but the next second he's got them bubbling away and I sink back in the water against his chest.

We were frantic earlier but now our movements are languid, like we're both moving in slow motion.

His hands, so brutal only fifteen minutes earlier, are now gentle and soothing as he runs soap down my bare shoulders. He lathers the soap and then cups my breasts and runs his thumbs over my nipples.

I can't help arching into his touch and I feel his erection stir back to life beneath me. I'm not sure I can handle another round at this point, it's so intense with him, but when he gently moves my hair off my shoulder and his lips come to the nape of my neck with whisper kisses, I melt back against him.

I move restlessly in the water against him, rubbing my ass against his cock. Shit, I'm not sure what I'm doing but I suddenly can't think of anything other than having him inside me again. Maybe I don't know what I'm asking for. I'm sore down there and I can't do any more anal—

But when he reaches down and guides himself inside me, it's into my pussy. And he doesn't do it roughly.

For the first time, he's gentle.

He wraps his arms around me, the side of his face pressed against the back of my neck and shoulder and he breathes roughly into my ear, "What the hell are you doing to me?"

He fucks me slow and deep, the already roiling water sloshing slightly more with his movements.

And *oh*—

The fullness of him.

The rightness of it.

I let out a little keening cry and he twists one of my nipples. I hiss and he pinches it harder while reaching to stroke my clit with his other hand.

I cry out in pleasure while he drops kisses along my shoulder. "You're so fucking beautiful," he whispers. "So fucking perfect."

And then I'm crying again. But not because it hurts. Or maybe it does. Hearing those words that are always so impossible for me to believe, from him, in this moment with everything stripped down between us.

Does he know what he's doing to me?

Does he know that in this moment he could break me with a single word?

Because right now, right here, I'm raw.

This is the same place Bryce Gentry used to take me. But after Bryce got me here, he never told me I was perfect.

He brought me to my most vulnerable and then let me know how worthless I was. Useless. Ugly. Cheap. Over and over. He took me to the brink and then instead of lifting me up, he'd stomp me under his heel.

But when Dylan cups my face so that I'm looking back at him, his eyes are full of the wonder from earlier.

He swallows hard, not uttering a word as his eyes search mine. That's when I see it. I'm not the only one raw right now. I'm not the only one cut open like a heart patient on the operating table with their ribs spread wide.

I reach a hand around to touch his face, too. I scrape my thumb down the stubble on his jaw. I run my forefinger across the slight lines on his forehead. He can't yet be thirty but he looks older. Weary beyond his years.

He snatches my hand and brings it to his lips, kissing my knuckles. And then he sucks my fingers into his mouth, all the while moving slowly but forcefully inside me.

I shudder and feel my eyelids flutter closed.

Oh *God*.

I thought hard and brutal was the best sex I'd ever had but *this*? This passionate, slow intensity?

"Eyes," he demands.

My eyes spring open and go back to his. He doesn't offer more. He just holds my hand to my shoulder, a subtle sort of bondage, and I kept my head twisted round to look at him.

The position makes my neck ache and eventually I have to look away.

But Dylan's not having that. He lifts me off of him and moves us in the tub, twisting me so that I'm facing him, my legs straddling him. We're no longer along the back of the tub but in the center.

His cock nudges at the lips of my sex and slips back in like it knows exactly where home is. I can't help grinding down on him, rubbing my pelvis to get friction exactly where I need it most.

He hisses and grasps my shoulders from behind, pulling me down as far as possible on his cock.

Then he loops one arm around my waist and uses the buoyancy of the water to help lift me up. He pulls me back down and I squeeze my walls as tight around him as possible. The corresponding strain on his face is so satisfying I concentrate all my strength on my core, squeezing and tightening with every downstroke.

"Fuck," he hisses low right before he tangles his hand in my hair again and drags me down for a passionate kiss.

I cry out against his mouth as, once more, my pleasure ramps up. He bites and licks and teases at my tongue and lips. It's more of a give and take than it was earlier. And he must be learning my body, because as my breaths grow shorter and higher pitched, he pulls away, watching me with an expression I can't read.

The moment my orgasm, pleasure also strains his face as his mouth drops open and he shoves into me and then he's cumming.

For a single second, we're both lost in pleasure. The pleasure we've gifted to one another.

And in that moment, I know perfection.

But the next one is pretty damn good, too, because even though I gasp as the white light recedes and the world comes back into focus, it's to Dylan's strong arms around me and Dylan's mouth on mine again.

He kisses me the entire time he reaches to unplug the bathtub stopper. And he kisses me while we both clumsily stand up in the tub. He breaks our kiss only for a moment while he steps out and reaches for towels.

But the second he shoves mine into my hands, he has his hands in my wet hair and he's pulling me to him and kissing me again.

I giggle and he grins as he helps me out of the tub.

And then he's got his arms wrapped around me, the towel trapped between us while we both drip water onto the bathroom tile.

I break away laughing and gasping for breath. "I don't think this is going to get us dry."

"I don't fucking care," is all he growls before pulling me back and kissing me again. It's like he's a man starved. Like he's been walking through the desert and I'm the first tall glass of water he's had in weeks.

And um, yeah, I can't say I exactly mind.

The last time I kissed anyone this much was... high school? And back then it was fumbling and terribly awkward making out with a high school boyfriend.

But Dylan doesn't kiss like a boy just learning his way around a girl.

No, Dylan kisses like a man.

And when he drags me over to the bed, his hands move over my body the way a man's hands do on a woman.

As does his mouth.

Oh God, his *mouth*.

"We're wet," I try to protest.

"Oh you'll be wet," he murmurs as he crawls down my body and then his tongue teases a circle around my clitoris.

I should be completely sexed out after cumming... how many times have I already cum tonight? I've lost count. But when begins lapping and sucking hungrily at my clit, then biting, I cum again with a howl.

Though I do have to admit, his satisfied grin when he moves back up my body does have a bit of the schoolboy in it.

"Proud of yourself, are you?" I arch an eyebrow.

He shrugs, his grin growing wider. But then he's all seriousness as he moves on top of me, mouth devouring mine again. I can taste myself on his tongue, and holy *Jesus*, I wouldn't have thought that would be as hot as it is.

And minutes later, his erection is growing hard against my leg.

I pull back from him, eyes wide. "*Again?*"

His reaching down and guiding himself inside me is his only answer.

CHAPTER SEVEN

DYLAN

"What's the problem if the bitch likes it?" Bryce asked, laughing as he grabbed the hair of the blonde girl giving him head and shoving her further down his cock.

She gagged and struggled in his grasp and my stomach went tight but I couldn't look away. "I don't know. I'm not sure she likes it."

I also wasn't sure if I wanted to rip Bryce's hands off the girl and help her to the elevator and out of the building or if I wanted to rip Bryce's hands off the girl and shove her down on my own cock. Fuck, even the thought—I've been stiff for the last fifteen minutes ever since Bryce texted her and she came right over. He ordered her on her knees and she's been there ever since while we kept on gaming and talking.

Bryce was cool. I met him an MIT Alumni dinner where he and I started chatting. He was like me. He was making shit happen even though he was in his mid-twenties. His company was already gaining recognition and getting international tech contracts. We were the new fucking generation in tech and we were gonna be the next power players.

But Bryce worked hard and played harder. The more I hung out with him, the more I saw shit like this. The wild parties he threw, the way he treated the girls he always had around—

Bryce rolled his eyes and pulled the blonde girl up by her hair. She winced in pain and there were tears in her eyes. "Do you want to leave?" he snapped at her.

She shook her head quickly.

"Then what the fuck are you doing? Suck my fucking cock!" With that, Bryce shoved her back down on his dick.

I frowned even as my cock gave a little jolt in my pants. Bryce just laughed. "Lighten the fuck up. Jesus. You're only twenty-three. Besides, you already told me you had a good time at my party the other night."

I can't help nodding at that. Fuck yeah I had a good time the other night. A disturbingly good time. That girl had been like this one, passive and willing to do whatever Bryce demanded.

The question was, *why*? Were they just into kink, like Bryce said? The girl sucking Bryce's cock right now didn't seem to be having a very good time.

Bryce reassured me earlier that neither this girl or the girl from the other night was a prostitute. I think I might have felt better if they were. That would have at least made sense to me. They'd be getting something out of it I could understand. Then I could get why they stayed.

I put my hand to the back of my neck uncomfortably and then pulled out my phone. "I gotta bounce. Promised my sister I'd take her out to the movies."

Bryce choked out a laugh. "You'd rather babysit than get a blow job? You know I always share. I was gonna give you the bitch when she's done with me."

I just shook my head.

"Damn. You got a warped sense of priorities, brother."

I rolled my eyes as I left. Bryce was cool but he could be a real dick sometimes. Didn't mean I wasn't thinking about the girl sucking him off as I drove home. Was he fucking her now? She was probably a slut if she just came over and immediately dropped to her knees to suck him off like that. Dad was always warning me to watch out for weak-willed sluts who'd be after me just for the family money.

Like Mom.

I frowned. I didn't like to think about Mom like that but Dad called her a money-grubbing slut often enough. When I was young, every time there'd be some really ugly scene, Dad would buy her some new jewelry. I'd always hear her brag about it to her friends, how he still doted on her and then she'd show off the new diamond bracelet or ring or earrings.

Why else had she stayed all these years and put up with Dad's shit? Did she stay just because of the prenup? She lost everything if she left him. Or did she, in some twisted way, *like* what he did to her?

Her obsession the past few years had become plastic surgery instead of diamonds and I'd heard her scream, *Not in the face!* one time when dad was wailing on her, like they had some pact where he wouldn't hit her in her brand new face.

I was sixteen and I ran in when she screamed. Dad was fucking her. I ran at his back and wrestled him off her. I'd just hit a growth spurt and I was finally big enough to take him on. But Dad wouldn't fight me. He just shoved me off him.

Ask the slut if she wants it, was all he'd said.

And I'd turned to Mom. She'd pulled her skirt down and her head was bowed. *Mom, I'll get you out of here. Let's go*, I begged. *Right now. You don't have to stay here with this—*

But she just cut me off. *Enough. I'm fine, Dylan. Leave us alone. Now. Don't try to get involved in things you don't understand.*

Mom—

Get out of here!

I ran but I didn't make it out of the front door before I heard dad start up again, rutting her like she was a common whore.

I hadn't understood it back then. I thought dad was just a monster. But now, thinking back to the woman from Bryce's party the other night... That chick was one hot piece of ass and she'd gotten off on everything we'd done to her. A room full of guys. And she just kept *cumming*, no matter what we did. Spanking. Slapping her tits. Spitting. She fucking loved all of it.

I'd left early but today, before the blonde got there, Bryce showed me footage taken that night. Bryce said the video was from the end of the night, long after I'd left. The girl had looked like a broken doll, so worn out she couldn't even get up on her knees anymore. But when Bryce fucked her, hard, using her body more roughly than any porno I'd ever seen, she *still came*.

So maybe some bitches really did just like it like that.

Fuck, even thinking about it now was enough to make me hard. I frowned deeper as I adjusted myself and pulled into the garage of our family house. The only time I ever came by here anymore was to hang out with my little sister. I looked through some baseball stats on my phone till my stiffy was gone, then hopped out of my car and went inside looking for Chloe.

The garage entrance was close to the kitchen, so I popped in and grabbed an apple, calling out, "Chloe?" and taking a big bite of the crisp fruit. It was October and the apple was hard and sweet.

I chewed and swallowed, walking through the first floor with its lofty ceilings. All the white furniture was spotless, as always. Not a piece out of place. Nor any evidence that any humans actually lived there. Just like Mom liked it.

"Mom? Chloe?"

I turned around after checking in the TV room and finding it empty.

Jesus this place was lifeless. I should call Dare and make him come over for dinner sometime this week. We saw or Skyped each other almost every day as we were getting Lennox Brothers off the ground. We'd almost finished getting our first round of investor funding. Darren was the charismatic face of the company and I was the engineering brains.

But more than that, it was really fucking cool to get to know my brother as a man. We'd lost touch for a few years there while I was out on the east coast at MIT and he went to Stanford. But he was a good guy and well... it meant a lot to me to be able to build a business with someone from my *family*. Someone from my family I wasn't ashamed of.

Not to mention, Dare didn't just know how to work hard, he knew how to have fun—something I wasn't always the best at. He helped me not take life so damn seriously all the time.

But while things between me and Darren were better than ever, Chloe was still stuck here in this house with my parents. She deserved more than a once a month drop in from her oldest brother. Dare and I should be coming by for dinner once a week. Maybe on Sundays. Just to make sure Dad wasn't getting too out of line and to make sure she was doing good in school. *And* to double check there weren't any boys sniffing around.

Sure, she could start dating *eventually*. Maybe when she was like thirty-five.

I headed upstairs. Chloe was probably in her room with her noise-canceling headphones on, watching YouTube, totally lost to the world.

I smiled and shook my head as I jogged up the last of the stairs and turned the corner.

And heard a muffled scream. But this time, it wasn't Mom. It was too high-pitched. Girlish.

"Chloe!" I yelled, sprinting for her door at the end of the hallway. "Chloe!"

But her door was locked.

Her door was locked and I couldn't get to her.

"Chloe!" I screamed again, throwing my shoulder against the door. "*CHLOE!*"

"Dylan. Dylan! Wake *up*!"

Someone's trying to hold me back from getting to her, arms around my chest trying to hold me back. No. "Chloe!"

I fight until I hear a female cry of pain that has me freezing and blinking in confusion. Wait, wha—

I'm not in my parent's house. I'm not— I'm not—

I look around in confusion.

And see Miranda with eyes as wide as saucers, holding her arm to her chest like— Like it was hurt. Oh Jesus fuck, like *I* hurt her—

"Dylan," she whispers. "Who's Chloe?"

I have to get the fuck out of here.

Now.

I whip the sheets off of me and head for the door, grabbing my clothes and stumbling into my pants as I go.

I should never have listened to Dr. Laghari. What the fuck was I *thinking*? I'm so fucking *stupid*. I'm a fucking monster exactly like Dad. That'll never change. It's in my fucking DNA. The first woman I try to get close to in years and she ends up— Jesus, I couldn't even go one *night* without hurting her.

"Dylan," she calls after me. "Dammit, Dylan!"

She's fast and she catches up to me before I can get to the front door. She scurries around me and blocks the door with her body.

"What the fuck?" she asks, eyes blazing in the light of the kitchen we never turned off earlier. She didn't bother to throw anything on so she's still completely naked. She's absolutely fucking glorious.

And not for you.

I avert my eyes. "I have to go." I say it in a tone that brooks no argument and reach around her for the doorknob but she blocks my hand with her hip.

"The fuck you do. What was that about? You had a nightmare. That's all."

What the fuck— Is she really going to stand there and deny that I — "I hurt you!"

"On accident! While you were asleep." She throws her hands up in exasperation. "So next time I won't body wrestle you to wake you up if you're having a nightmare. You flail. It's understandable. Lesson learned."

But I'm already shaking my head. She doesn't understand. I'm a violent man. Dangerous. Jesus Christ, didn't she learn anything from the first night we met?

What the fuck time is it anyway? A quick glance toward the window shows it's still dark out.

"I have to go," I say, voice icy. "This was a mistake. One that won't happen again."

She scoffs. "You said that the first time, remember?"

I breathe out in frustration. What the hell can I say that will get her to move?

I'm about two seconds from bodily lifting her out of the way when suddenly she stops blocking the door and instead slips her arms around my waist. She squeezes me and buries her head against my chest.

Instead of obstinate, her voice is soft when she whispers, "I'm sorry you had a nightmare. I'm so sorry. It sounded horrible. You don't have to, but I'm here to listen if you want to talk about it."

Then she squeezes me tight again, like she's using all her strength. I– I– No one's— I stumble a step backwards and she just follows, still hugging me.

No one's hugged me like this since Chloe.

I choke as I try to swallow hard at the thought.

I don't deserve—

But at the same time it feels so good. *Welcome home*, her embrace seems to say.

NO. This isn't how— I need to *leave*.

But she just keeps hugging me and after several more long seconds, my arms that have been stiff hovering in the air finally settle down around her.

The second I do, it's like my body has a mind of its own. It sinks against her like candle wax melting into a mold.

A Miranda shaped mold.

And it's more than on the outside.

Every space she's empty, I want to fill. It's a longing so fierce and sudden, I feel a little short of breath.

What the fuck am I doing?

Am I coming or going? I don't fucking know.

Going. You should be going. You'll only hurt her in the end. More than you already have.

But when she whispers, "Come back to bed," I can only shake my head.

I feel her disappointment when she whispers, "oh," and her shoulders fall. But it's only because she's misunderstood me.

I quickly clarify by cupping her cheeks and lifting her face to me, exposing that mouth that I'm becoming fucking addicted to.

I kiss her and she's just as sweet as earlier when I couldn't get enough of her. The way she kisses. It's like she's surprised every time, opening her mouth on a gasp to me. Her tongue is questioning and eager against mine and it drives me fucking crazy.

I push her up against the door she was blocking and grab both her arms, slamming them to the wood up above her head.

I'm hard again. Somehow. Christ knows I could never go this many times in one night back before my self-imposed bout of celibacy. Maybe it's just because my dick is excited to be near a flesh and blood woman again but no, I know it's more than that.

It's *her*.

With the hand not holding her wrists, I reach down and grab her buttocks, squeezing hard and then giving a sharp *smack*. She yelps and arches her breasts into my chest.

I didn't have time to actually button my slacks earlier which is good because I can't stand another second not being inside her.

I jerk my pants down over my ass and then hike her up against the door, impaling her ruthlessly the next second.

I feel her full body shudder as she arches into me even further.

"*Yesssss*," she hisses.

Yes.

She's not saying no or even pretending to struggle. But I'm still hard. Rock hard with no sign of it changing any time soon.

I pull back from her, breathing hard as I look at her in confusion. What does it mean? Could she be— Could she *cure* me? Could I finally have sex without needing to—

She doesn't seem to be in the mood for deep thought at the moment, though, because she dips her head to kiss me again, biting at my bottom lip and digging her fingers into my hair, nails dragging down my scalp.

Fuck but she's so goddamned hot.

I pull out and then slam in again, rattling the door in its frame with the force of my thrust. She only wraps her legs around me and squeezes around my shaft harder. Jesus Christ but I've never been with anyone who could—

I let out a low growl and thrust my tongue back in her mouth. I have one hand under her thigh to support her but I drop the other one down as well. This one I reach further around.

And shove a finger up her ass.

Her entire body reacts. It's like I just jabbed her with a cattle prod, she's so sensitive back there after I reamed her out earlier. Just the thought sends satisfaction rumbling throughout my body and my cock gets stiffer.

So much for being cured.

But as deep inside her as I am, I can't give a fuck.

So I shove a second finger inside her backside and love how her grasp around my neck tightens. It's more like she's holding on for dear life now.

Like I'm her bouy in a storm—even though I *am* the storm.

I lose it. Absolutely fucking lose it.

I fuck her ruthlessly. And I don't come quick. I draw it out. Long minutes fucking her up against the door. Five minutes. Ten.

We're both sweating. I work out five times a week and still my muscles are straining to the max but I don't want to stop.

I want to take Miranda there. To the brink. I want to push her. I want to hurt her. To break and remake her. I want everything she fucking has.

I take her to the edge of coming and when she's about to go over, I still all my movements, leaving her frustrated. Over and over and over until she's crying and begging and exhausted with fucking.

And then and only then do I give it to both of us

In one last burst of strength, I pull back and then slam her repeatedly against the door, grinding my hips and swirling to give her the satisfaction she's been craving.

She comes with a high-pitched cry, tears streaming down her cheeks as she buries her head against my neck. I pump into her, finally allowing my own release as well.

I'm all but dizzy as I use the very last of my strength to carry her back to the bedroom and we both collapse exhausted into bed. And I mean fucking *exhausted*. Worn out, soul spent, exhausted. But it's a *clean* tired, which might sound funny, cause that sex was dirty and hot as fucking hell.

But shit, I can't even think any more, because I swear Miranda just sucked out my life force through my dick and I crash to the pillow.

I thought after all that I'd be out like a light.

And maybe I do fall asleep for a few minutes.

Miranda is stroking her fingers through my hair. Somehow instead of ending up with her in my arms, I've ended up in hers, my head on her ample chest.

Maybe some part of me is too wary of falling back asleep again, though. What if I have another nightmare? The second the thought passes through my brain, I instantly become more alert.

I can hear her heartbeat thudding through her chest and it's so... nice. Peaceful. I've never laid like this with a woman before.

So many firsts with this woman.

She keeps stroking my hair and I think any second she'll stop, that she'll drop off to sleep, but her breathing never slows or evens out.

I settle in, soothed like a beast by her petting.

"You're good at that," I murmur.

She laughs and I love the way I can feel it rumbling throughout her body.

"You have good hair," she says, grazing her nails gently along my scalp before rubbing circles at my temples with her thumbs.

We don't say anything else for long minutes. Her touch is too soothing. It would be too easy to drop back off to sleep and I can't fucking do that.

The image of her holding her arm to her chest flashes through my head. Followed by another image—my sister, curled in a ball on her bed. I'm instantly more awake.

Eventually her hand slows, she finally stops stroking my hair, and I hear her breathing ease.

But I don't allow myself to fall back asleep for the rest of the night. I checked the clock beside her bed. She set it for six-thirty. I slip out of her house at six-twenty-five after one last, lingering look at the woman who is far, *far* too good for me.

If I were any kind of honorable man, I'd never look back.

CHAPTER EIGHT

DYLAN

Three days.

I make it three whole days without responding to Miranda's text.

I can't imagine what she must have thought, waking up after the night we had and finding herself alone in bed.

Hopefully she thought *he's an asshole who's not worth my time.*

Her text came right when her alarm went off and she found me gone.

It said, simply: *Please don't run.*

Followed a few minutes later by: *I could be your safe place.*

That one text gutted me. Because fuck, I know it's true. I felt it that night. I felt the kind of safety I haven't since... well I'm not sure I ever felt as safe as I did last night. Certainly not when I was a kid. I could never truly relax in that house. I always had to be on edge for the next time Dad's voice would be raised or time Mom screamed out in pain. Get the kids out of the house. Don't let them see. Protect them. Protect—

And look how well that worked out.

I've been having the nightmare every night since I left Miranda's. And it's as vivid as the first time I lived through it all.

There are the sounds I'll never forget. Chloe's screams. My fist banging uselessly at the door.

Someone was hurting her. Violating her, and I couldn't get through. Not in time to help her. Not in time to be any good to anybody.

Of course the terrible, terrible truth was that I was years too late.

Even though I'm at work and am wide awake, the flashbacks are so real I might as well be reliving them.

I slammed my shoulder against the door a second time and the door finally gave way. Only to find my sister weeping on the bed, tugging down the skirt of her school uniform as the door to her bathroom shut behind someone exiting out the bedroom.

"You son of a bitch!" I shouted, sprinting across the room and yanking the door open. The bathroom had two doors because it was shared between bedrooms and I ran for the other one. I'd kill the motherfucker when I caught him. I'd fucking kill h—

I yanked the door open.

Only to find my father in his dressing gown, standing with his hands out. "Dylan, now just wait a second. You—"

"You sick fuck!" I shouted and ran at him.

My first punch had him on the floor. He'd been a powerful man once but a heart attack last year had left him weakened.

Not so weak he couldn't still prey on his own daughter. I was going to throw up. How could—? How long had he—?

I reared back and punched him again. He shoved at me even as blood spurted from his nose but I didn't care.

Chloe. Sweet Chloe. She was the best of us. The only good thing to come out of this house besides Darren.

"Dylan. Dylan!"

The shrieks from the other room came through my haze of fury only distantly at first but as soon as they registered, I dropped my father to the ground and stumbled backwards.

"Chloe?" I turned and ran back through the bathroom to her room.

She was still where I'd last seen her. On the bed, hunched over, except she'd pulled the blanket around her, only her head peeking out. It was something she used to do as a little girl when there was a thunderstorm.

Oh God. Oh Jesus. What had he done to her. What had he done?

"Chloe," I said, my voice and my heart breaking as I went to her. She flinched back as I got close and I froze.

Her eyes were red and puffy and she looked at the wall as she said, "Dylan, get me out of this place. No police. No custody bullshit." Her eyes finally came to mine and they were just... empty. "Get me out of here and don't tell dad or anyone else where you take me. Anyone. Do you understand me. Not Darren. Not Dad." She shuddered.

"Jesus, Chloe, I'd never tell Dad."

I took another step toward her and again she flinched. "Just get me out of here," she said, eyes jumping back toward the wall.

She couldn't even look at me.

She knew.

She knew I was like him. That even earlier this afternoon, I'd been thinking maybe that wasn't such a bad thing. Jesus, I needed to throw up. I needed to kill my father.

But I needed to get her out of this house more.

I swallowed down the bile creeping up my throat. "Do you want to change or pack a bag?"

Her eyes darted over to me and then away again. She shook her head. "Just get me out of here."

I nodded stiffly, trying for her sake to keep my shit together.

She got up from the bed, still with the blanket around her. She held it like it was a shield even though both of us knew it had done nothing to protect her that day.

Just like I hadn't.

"Dylan, what the hell, man?"

I jerk my head up to see Darren standing in the door of my office.

"You're the one who called this meeting and you're standing me up?"

"Shit." I look down at the time on my computer and realize it's ten minutes after two. I push my chair back and hurry to my feet, looking around and trying to grab the appropriate papers. And my laptop. Shit, don't forget the laptop—

"Christ, slow down," Darren laughs, coming in and helping me with the papers. "We're the CEO and CFO. Believe me. The meeting won't start without us."

I cringe. I hate to be *that guy*. The boss that demands a standard from everybody else he doesn't adhere to himself. And I'm pretty big on punctuality.

I swing my laptop bag over my shoulder.

"Okay, I've got everything. Let's go."

Dare just keeps shaking his head. "Slow down, take a breath. I know all the sudden you've decided to start taking a more active role in the company again, but the world won't stop spinning if Dylan Lennox pauses to take a breath every so often."

He claps me on the back and I do what he says, take a big breath in.

Yes, I do want to be more active again. Of course Darren noticed that I wasn't living up to my end of the bargain when it's come to being an equal partner in the company. I've walked around Lennex Brothers Corp like a zombie for years. But that's all changing.

Ever since meeting Miranda, it's like I was asleep for a hundred years and I'm just now waking up.

And it feels fucking terrifying. I'm not used to...*feeling* this much. To seeing this much.

For example, Lennox Bros. is about to launch a new robotics board in six months. And we were all set to go.

But we were going about it all wrong—playing it safe when we needed to be pushing the limits of innovation.

Hence, the meeting I'd called and am now late for.

I take the lead out of my office and head down the hallway to the conference room. All the usual suspects are there. Rob, Darren's right hand man on the business end. Malik from engineering. Kayla from acquisitions. Natalie and several other reps handling the hardware bids. A handful of other people fill out the room. Water bottles are set out at each chair and a coffee tray steams on the back counter.

I sit at one head of the oval table and Darren takes the other.

"So," Darren waves at me as soon as we're settled. "We're on pins and needles. What's the reason for this meeting?"

Darren kept asking for a heads up to what the meeting was about but I wanted to wait and do it here. I'm not like Darren. I can't just talk off the cuff. I'm best when I have all my facts together and I've thought through the presentation I want to make.

I take another deep breath like Darren suggested earlier and then begin.

"Right now the robotics board we're about to push in six months is using the same kind of processor the last ten boards have used. But Intel-based processors are the past when it comes to robotics. They're slow and inefficient when it comes to the massive amount of real time data you're dealing with in robotics."

I open up my laptop and go over the statistics from the past few years. It's all clearer and clearer in my head the more I talk.

I finally look up at everyone again. "We don't want to just be *another* robotics company out there. That was never our goal. Lennox Brothers is about pushing the envelope, being *the best* robotics company in the Silicon Valley, always on the cutting edge."

I pause and look at each person, from face to face. "So I don't think we have any other choice but to switch to a RISC based processor with our next launch."

Talk immediately erupts around the table.

Kayla speaks up. "But we already have contracts in place with our current suppliers. We can't just—"

"We have *bids* from our current suppliers," I correct. "I checked and know for a fact that we haven't committed to anyone for the new line yet."

Kayla's mouth drops open but then she closes it again, looking to Darren. She's not the only one. About half the table is looking my brother's way, like they expect him to put a stop to what I'm saying or put me in line.

I frown. All *riiiiight*. Apparently more has slipped in the past few years than I realized. I am still the CEO.

But Dare has my back, just like always.

"I've been hearing murmurs about the RISC chips here and there," Darren says.

"It's more than murmurs," I say. "RISC chips reduce consumption and can work up to ten times faster than the old style of processors. Half the community is already convinced RISC chips are the future of robotics, and if we can be on the frontier of integrating—"

"What about the other half?" Rob cuts in. "Doesn't that mean that the other half thinks they're a bad idea? I mean, when did status quo become the bad guy? We did a seven *billion* dollar quarter last year. We should go with what we *know* works." He lets out a huffed laugh. "You don't gamble when it comes to seven billion dollars."

Who the fuck let this guy in here? This is a meeting about the product and he's some asshole in a suit.

"Yes," I say, conscious to stay absolutely calm on the outside. "But the reason we did that seven-billion-dollar quarter is because of our *product* and *brand*. Because people know they can trust that Lennox Brothers Robotics are always at the forefront of the state of the art. Our brand is everything. If we lose that confidence by putting out a product they can get anywhere else that's slower than our competitors, then—"

"How about this?" Darren interrupts me.

I glare his way but he puts out a pacifying hand and I can see from his look that he's pleading for me to hear him out.

Which is when I remember that yeah, while I've been checked out, it's Dare who's been steering this ship singlehandedly while I holed away down in in engineering and let the months and years pass me by.

I nod toward him and take my seat.

"My brother's right," Dare starts and I struggle not to smile at the reactions of the suits to his words. They all look like they're sucking on lemons.

"Lennox is all about consumer trust," Dare says, "and we can't break that by giving them anything other than the most superior product."

"But," he raises a hand again when it seems like he's going to get talk back, "we can only guarantee the most superior product if we can build it and get it working flawlessly. All the companies who've bid to have their processor used in our robotics board have sent along prototypes. So let's do extensive testing and let the data speak for itself.

Which processor gets the job done best in the fastest time? Let's find that out, and then make our decisions."

And *this* is why my brother is the face of Lennox Bros. Dare is so damn good with people. I assume that when I produce facts, that logical action will follow. I know the RISC processor will produce the best results without jumping through all the hoops of testing it against the others. But Darren sees what I can't—that to appease the suits, we'll need charts and defensible evidence to prove their money will be safe.

The rest of the meeting is logistics, organizing the order of testing the processors and which team leads will head up who, along with making a timeline. We won't have long, three weeks or a month at *most*, but that will be pushing it if we want to keep to our current production schedule, six months out.

Two hours later, the meeting breaks up and Darren shakes everyone's hand and chats as they all leave. I stay seated, phone in hand. Now that the meeting's over, I'm back to staring at Miranda's text.

I could be your safe place if you'd let me.

I shake my head and shove my phone in the side of my laptop bag, then I stand up to stretch my legs. Darren turns to me when the last person is finally gone.

"I could have used a heads up about this one."

"I'm sorry. You're right. I thought it would—" I gesture at the table and shake my head.

Dare frowns. "What?"

"Well I thought switching to the RISC chips was such an obvious move, I thought the meeting would just be about how to implement them. I didn't even think about pushback."

Darren busts out laughing at that. He's still shaking his head when he comes over to me and claps me on the back. "Christ, Dylan. I know you're my older brother, but I swear sometimes it's like I'm the one shielding you from the way the world really works. Change freaks people out. You have to go slow and then convince them it was their idea all along."

"Jesus, I hate all that politicking bullshit." I shake my head and take a swig from my water bottle.

"Which is why you tinker and build the nice machines and I sell them. Now, enough about work. Anything happen with the babe in the red dress?"

I choke on the water and spit half of it out.

"Whoa, whoa!" Darren smacks me on the back and I cough until I can finally manage a breath.

"Christ, that bad?" Darren laughs.

I shake my head, swiping my mouth on my shirt sleeve. After another few coughs to clear my throat, I look up only to find Darren with an eyebrow raised.

"So it went well? Let's hear it. Was she screaming your name or was it more of a dine and dash situation?"

I roll my eyes and grab my chest. "Jesus, I'm dying over here and all you can think about is whether or not I got laid?" The last thing I want to talk about is Miranda. I'm too fucked up about her in my own head to try to be able to make sense of it all in words, especially to Dare, who only sees women in terms of notches on his bed post.

"Basically." Darren nods. "Now, I gotta know. Were those tits real?"

"Jesus, Dare." Then I scrunch my forehead. "Wait, how do you even know about her?"

"I stopped by the conference."

"You hate those things."

"Not true." He holds up a finger. "I hate the boring as fuck *talks*. Now the partying afterward, that I'm all about. But right as I got off the elevator in the lobby from my room, I saw you following her out."

"You had a room at the hotel that night?"

"Yes. Unlike some people, when I see a woman I want, I'm not afraid to seal the deal." He scrutinizes me before a smile slowly creeps across his face. "You *did* it, didn't you? You dog." He raises both hands. "Well all I can say is hallelujah, praise Jesus. So all it took was a stacked brunette to finally bring an end to the—what? year long?—dry spell?"

More like six years, not that he ever needs to know. "Shut up, dumbass. And don't talk about her like that." Miranda is so much more than he's making her out to be. Even thinking about her hurts because it just reminds me of all I'll never have.

"Ooooh," he draws the word out. "So it's like that? Has there been a second date? Come on, I tell you everything. In the hotel, I took Rita, this hot as fuck piece of ass from Kent Laboratories, and fucked her brains out in the bathroom. She must do fucking gymnastics, because I had her bent so far over, I swear her—"

"Enough." I squeeze my eyes shut and put a hand to my temple. "How many times do I have to tell you that I don't want a play by play of your most recent fuck toy?"

"I figure I'm doing you a favor. You gotta have material for the spank bank somehow, right?"

"I'm done with this conversation," I start walking for the door.

Darren just laughs behind me. "Never gets old. You make it too easy, brother. And it's Friday night. Go live a little."

I roll my eyes but right before I get to the door, I stop, remembering what happened the last time I gave in and *lived a little*. Miranda, cradling her arm. And that was after we acted out a fantasy of me *raping* her.

Like father like son.

"Hey," I swallow down my self-disgust and turn my head back toward Darren, "do you ever miss Chloe?"

Darren's face sobers instantly and he blinks a couple times, obviously surprised by my non-sequitur. "Yeah, all the time. What makes you ask?"

I shrug and look down.

"Do you ever call her? Or write?"

After that horrific afternoon, I took Chloe straight to a hotel. She was only a few months away from her eighteenth birthday so I kept her hidden away in the hotel until then. Once she turned eighteen, I asked her where she wanted to live. She said Austin, so we bought plane tickets to Texas. I bought her a house there with my portion of my grandfather's inheritance I'd gotten when I'd turned eighteen.

She doesn't do social media so I can't look in on her. But I try to imagine her happy. Even though I know it's probably a fucking lie. After all she went through... for *years*... To this day, I don't know how many years my father sexually abused her.

Darren looks toward the window. "I tried. In the beginning."

I gave him her number and email right after she moved. I figured she should have some tie to the only part of her family that wasn't fucked up. Or that wasn't me. If there was one gift I could give my sister after all she went through, it was never having to see my face again.

I look exactly like my father.

Sometimes when I look in the mirror in the morning I feel a rush of rage and self-hatred so violent that I've broken at least two mirrors by punching them.

"Did she talk to you?"

Darren shakes his head. "It just went to voicemail. She never opened my emails, either."

I swallow and nod. "She needed a clean break."

"From *what*?" Darren looks at me and takes a step closer. "Dylan, *what happened*?"

The cocky, self-assured guy from minutes ago is gone. It's my little brother standing in front of me now. The same little brother who would grab hold of my legs and look up at me, eyes wide and scared when I ushered him and Chloe out to the back yard after Dad started yelling and I knew what would follow.

"I know it was something bad," he says. "Something with Dad. And Chloe. He was never the same after she left and then just months later he had another heart attack when he'd been doing fine for years." He gets right in my face. "I'm not stupid. I knew what went on in that house. Dad hit her, didn't he? He hit Chloe and you found out? Then you got her out of there?"

I turn away from him again and he grabs my shoulder in an iron grip, swinging me back around to look at him. "Stop it. I'm not a little kid anymore. You don't have to protect me."

"Yes I do!" I shout, shoving him off me. "I do." I back away, shaking my head. "I do. Believe me, it's better this way."

It's better if he never has that image in his head. So much better if all he has are suspicions that Dad hit Chloe. Jesus if only it had been that. If I can save him from the sick details of what actually happened, then by fuck, I will, no matter the cost.

"I'll see you on Monday," I mutter and stride out the door and into the hallway.

Still, his voice carries. "So you're just going to run away? Dylan."

Please don't run.

I squeeze my eyes shut after I punch the down button on the elevator.

I could be your safe place.

She's wrong. She's so wrong.

No place is safe.

Because the memories and the monsters?

They follow me wherever I go.

CHAPTER NINE

MIRANDA

"I don't need a man anyway," I shout to be heard above the club music, sloshing margarita over the edge of my cup. It spills down my fingers. "Oh, shit."

I giggle and slurp the frozen margarita slush that's slipping down my wrist.

Daniel rolls his eyes and leans in to shout so I can hear him. "You are a mess and you *so* need a man."

My mouth drops open as my eyes shoot back to Daniel. "Do not even start with me."

Daniel just crosses his arms over his chest and lifts one eyebrow like, oh yeah? "Then why are you wearing that little black dress and flashing so much thigh half the club is fucking you with their eyes? Plus, you only drink tequila when you're hoping to get some."

"Wha—? I am *not*." I jerk down on the hem of my dress. Okay so the dress might be a *tad* on the teensy side. "And everyone knows Chandelier has the best tasting Margaritas this side of Market street."

"Uh huh."

I make a face at him, then look around. "Where's Irina, anyway? Shouldn't she be here and, I don't know, like putting you in chastity or whipping your ass for even looking at these other women?"

Daniel gives a long-suffering sigh. "I wish. I ordered these new specialty silver ball crushers I've been wanting to try out with her but she just says she's been *busy* all week so we've only been able to play over Skype. If I just wanted to shove a dildo up my own ass and spank myself, I wouldn't need her in the first place. But that shit barely gets me off. It's fucking ridiculous."

Daniel is my best friend and one dirty mofo. I've watched him scene a few times at The Dungeon. He loves all aspects of being dominated by women. Well, as long as that woman is a serious sadist. Nobody loves pain like my boy Daniel.

I might like to ride the edge, but Daniel has never seen a cliff he doesn't want to jump off of, and has pushed things so far in bad situations that he's ended up in the hospital a couple times. But that's part of it for him. Trying to push his Dommes past their limits. Which means, really, it's him that's not the true sub, not me.

Or maybe it just means we're both really fucked up in our own delightful ways.

I put a hand on Daniel's arm. "I'm sorry, babe."

"Eh, it'll be fine." He shrugs it off but I can see he's still bothered. Daniel's the kind of guy who bottles things up and if he doesn't get release regularly, shit can get scary.

We met during one of his brief stints with therapy. It was after everything with Bryce and yeah, I wanted to die.

Daniel and I met in a group for people recovering from domestic abuse. It didn't feel like exactly the right word for what Bryce had done to me. What I'd *let* him do to me.

I never spoke up in group.

The stories the others told… they'd been married or in relationships with men who beat and raped them on a regular basis. Some of their partners apologized or bought flowers and were kind to them for a time, but always the violence came back. Most had been to the hospital more than once. One woman's arm was broken and she couldn't speak because her jaw had to be wired shut after her husband had broken it.

Their cases seemed so much more... I don't know, clean cut than mine? With Bryce it was more like—like I'd *participated* in the abuse, if that makes any sense.

I hated it but I still got off on it. By the end, I started craving it as my world narrowed down to a single focus—pleasing Bryce.

Even though pleasing him was impossible. Bryce was never pleased. Not by me, anyway. Not even by my suffering. I understood in the end that that was what he'd gotten off on all along. He wasn't capable of caring about anyone besides himself.

The only person in the group who spoke about anything close to what I'd experienced was Daniel.

He was only nineteen and had nothing like the physique he does today. He was rail-thin back then, a recovering addict, and only there because it was part of his court-ordered therapy after he stabbed his uncle in the thigh. He'd been aiming for the groin but his uncle had jumped away at the last second. An uncle who had brutally abused him for years after his mom died.

Daniel fluctuated between a sarcastic fuck-off attitude in therapy and rage-filled outbursts. I liked him immediately.

I approached him and asked him if he wanted to get coffee one night after he'd gone on a ten-minute rant about how he wished he'd killed his uncle instead of just stabbing him in the stupid leg.

Daniel looked me up and down. "What, is this like a sex thing? You want to fuck me cause you get off on sad, fucked up guys? Cause I'm down but only if you know how to swing a paddle."

"No, I don't want to—! God, I know you're an asshole, but maybe turn it off for like five minutes? Or half an hour to come have some damn coffee with me. As a friend," I emphasized. *"No sex. No,"* I shuddered, *"Paddles."*

He started laughing. Hard. Then pointing at me. "Jesus, you should see the look on your face."

I grabbed his finger he was pointing at me with and jammed it backwards until he jumped away. "Ow, ow, shit." Then he grinned at me. "You sure about the paddles? Cause that was a pretty good start."

I rolled my eyes and called over my shoulder that my invitation would be revoked if he didn't hurry his ass up.

And that was the start of our beautiful friendship.

"Do you want to dance?" Daniel asks suddenly and stands up. "Cause I don't want to sit here like two sad shits whining about not having a date."

I brighten and shove my phone into the side of my bra, then I extend my hand. "Yes. Let's dance."

He grins and pulls me onto the dance floor, immediately whirling me into a spin. My giggling shriek is lost in the pounding base of the club beat.

God, how long has it been since I just let loose and had *fun?*

It feels good not to worry about moody men with enigmatic pasts or to be anxious about keeping secrets of my own. The up-tempo beat slows to a mesmerizing, drumming base that thumps while a woman with an ethereal alto sings over top.

I hold onto Daniel's shoulders and sway with the music. My eyes fall shut and I lean my head backwards, shaking my long hair until I feel it swish back and forth against my shoulderblades.

The woman's sonorous, voice draws a long, sensuous note and I roll my head along with her voice, imagining it's Dylan's shoulders I'm clinging too, not Daniel's.

I whip my head back up and lean into his chest.

But the scent is all wrong. And the way he holds me, loosely around my waist.

Dylan always grips me, possessively, riding the edge of pinching. When I'm with Dylan, there's not a moment I can forget who I'm with.

Which is maybe why the last few days have felt so empty and colorless without him. I drop my forehead to Daniel's chest and his arms close around me.

"It's too bad you don't like beating the shit out of people," he says into my ear. "You and I would have made the best couple."

That makes me laugh and pull back. "Two subs together? Yeah, that never would have worked. It's why we've been able to be friends all these years."

Daniel smiles back. "I know, peanut. But alas, you aren't a mean enough bitch for me."

He kisses my forehead and then swings me out again. I squeal with laughter as he yanks me back into his chest. I always do, every time he pulls that move. Probably why he keeps doing it any time we find ourselves on a dance floor together. He loves making me laugh and he always knows when I need it.

He does some fancy jazz moves, dancing around me, completely ignoring the tempo of the music. He grabs my hands and we dance double tempo to the music, laughing and probably pissing off all the couples around us who are looking for a romantic moment.

We dance for another few songs until I grab Daniel's sleeve and go up on tiptoe so he can hear me over the thumping bass. "I need to go to the restroom."

"What?" he shouts, holding a hand to his ear.

"I need to pee."

"Huh?"

"I gotta piss!"

And naturally I shouted that when there was a short lull in the music and everyone around us turns my way.

Daniel just grins like the evil shit he is. I punch him in the shoulder and head for the bathrooms.

I smooth my hair down as I head for the hallway back to the restrooms. Damn, I'm thirsty. I should get some water. And order another margarita while I'm at it because I'm coming down off the nice floaty buzz and I—

What—?

I screech as I'm grabbed and roughly jerked sideways into a dark room. The door to the hallway I'm in slams shut and the next thing I know, I'm shoved face first against a wall.

"You think that's cute? To rub up against another man like that? To be a fucking cock tease?"

It's Dylan's voice.

My eyelids flutter shut as his big, manly hand shoves my little black dress up and palms my ass. Then he smacks it. So hard I cry out.

But it doesn't matter. The music is so loud in the club, no one can hear me.

"A tease is a promise, slut. And you owe me. You owe me big for that fucking show you were putting on out there."

The way he shoves his groin into my ass, it's clear how he means for me to pay up.

Why is he here?

The way he left things, God, I should be bitching him out. Demanding answers. He doesn't call. He doesn't text. Then he just shows up here and he has the audacity to be *jealous*!

Or maybe that's just part of the act? Has he even thought of me the past three days, when I've been a mess over him?

"If I was teasing anyone," I turn and say over my shoulder, "it was Daniel, not *you*. Not some fucking creeper hiding in the shadows just watching. I want a real man."

"This real enough for you?" he growls, shoving me down to the ground. It's pitch black and as my palms hit the tile floor, the smell of lemon-scented cleaners gets even stronger and—is that a mop bucket my shoulder just bumped into?

I don't have a chance to reach around to orient myself, though, because he lands on top of me. I cry out when he puts his knee in my back to hold me in place while he rips my panties down.

He shifts and the next second, I feel it, his fat cock shoving between my thighs.

I fight and twist underneath him but he leans over, caging me in.

"You want out, little girl, say the magic word." His breath is hot on my cheek.

But he knows, he has to know—that's the last thing in the world that I want. It doesn't mean I'm going down without a fight, though.

He. Didn't. Fucking. Call.

All week I've been going crazy thinking I was alone in this. Thinking that I'd blown it. I ran over every little thing I did and envisioned doing it differently. Anything to make an outcome where he ended up beside me in my bed when the alarm went off.

But he was, what? Just playing with me? Or maybe he thought *I* was the one playing. God, the way he found me in the garage with that random guy the first night we met... What if he really thinks I am a whore? That I spread it for anyone who'll spank me and say *yes* when I say *no*?

And tonight here I am, out with Daniel. But he's just a friend. I don't care what it looked like. I'm allowed to have friends.

"I am *not* a whore." I fight against Dylan's iron grip.

He reaches his other hand underneath me to lift my stomach up off the ground so that I'm slightly up on my knees.

"Oh yeah?" My entire body shudders when he reaches down, grabs his cock, and teases the head of it up and down my pussy lips. I can't help clenching and of course, he feels it.

He chuckles darkly.

"If you aren't a whore, why are you so wet for me? A creepy fucking stranger who was watching you all night?" He realigns his cock at the center of my core. "Or maybe *that's* what really gets you off. Imagining the men in the dark corners watching you and getting hard. Every one of them thinking about doing this."

He shoves into me and I screech. His hand slaps over my mouth. Every one of his moves is brutal. His hand mashes my mouth shut and each jerk of his hips as he fucks me is sharp and vicious.

"But I'm the only one who gets this cunt. I'm the only fucking one, do you hear me?"

Tears squeeze out of my eyes as I nod. Does he mean it? And how fucked up am I that his words are making me happy? But if he's the only one who gets to have me, it has to mean he wants me, right? That he wants there to be an *us*?

The next second though, all thoughts are obliterated when he shoves me off my knees so my belly is flush to the floor. My hands scrabble at the tiles but there's no getting away from him. His cock is so long and thick that even though my legs aren't spread, he has no problem continuing to fuck me.

And now, since the floor holds me completely still, he's able to fuck me even deeper, even harder.

He saws in and out of me and I can't remember the last time I was so thoroughly used. The orgasm is rising with each raw, harsh stroke.

"Jesus, Miranda," he says, pulling his hand away from my mouth, but only so he can grab my hair at the base of my neck. He drags my face sideways. If there were any light in this closet, I'd be able to see him over my shoulder. But as it is, it's still pitch black.

His voice, though, fills me with warmth and light.

"You're perfect, Miranda. The most perfect—" I don't know how he would have finished the thought because he crushes my mouth with his. His kiss is furious and demanding, and all the while he continues yanking my hair and fucking me.

The pain is perfect.

Just like him. I wasn't crazy about how good the other night was. This man. God, *this man*. I've never had perfect like him. Maybe I never will again.

Maybe there's only now, only this crescendo rising inside me. I break away from his mouth to let out the gasping whine.

Instead of kissing me again, though, he shoves two fat fingers into my mouth. I suck on them like I would his cock.

"Fuck," he calls and yanks my hair even harder. He's holding himself up by his elbows and I know the tile has to be punishing. How long can he keep this up?

I tease my teeth along his fingers stuffed in my mouth and he clutches my jaw with the rest of his hand.

My face is so small in his huge hand. He could crush me.

He rears back and then forces his fat cock back inside.

And I cum.

So hard and so long that I'm grateful for his fingers in my mouth because they muffle my howl.

It was his hand on my face that sent me over. Well, that and the fact that he's *really* fucking good at hitting just the right spot up so deep inside me. God, how does he do that?

But I know it's the thought that he could so easily break me—but he doesn't—that had me crying and choking his name around his fingers as the spasms hit.

He stills inside me right after I'm triggered. I clench around him as his cum spurts into me, even though it takes the very last of my strength to do it.

I've been sleeping for shit the past few nights and have been a zombie at work. But being here, with him, it's worth it. Anything is worth it as long as I have him.

I lift a hand behind me to cling to him as we both come down from the high.

We're both still dressed, connected only at our most intimate place. He stays hard inside me longer than anyone ever before and I love that he holds our connection long after the event has passed.

We linger and it's so damn beautiful.

He finally pulls his fingers out of my mouth and the hand that was ruthlessly gripping my hair only minutes ago now gently combs it back from my face.

I think I'm going to swoon from the gentleness.

Because it's dark and he can't see, I don't fight the tears that continue to flow down my cheeks. I don't want him to know this is the most intimate part yet.

That maybe even more than the sex, more than the pain, this is what I crave.

A soothing, loving touch from the same hand that brought the hurt.

This is what I *need*.

Both sides.

Jekyll and Hyde.

I need them both to love me.

Which is why I die, I *die*, when seconds later, he whispers, "shit," and jerks away from me. "Fuck, Miranda. This is wrong. I don't know why I— I was on my way home and that's where I should have gone. But then I remembered all those texts and worried you'd be waiting out back in the alley all alone."

Oh shit. The texts. I completely forgot about them. But he's right, I said I'd be waiting out back of the club tonight. I just figured, after the way we left things, he wouldn't want—

"And then you *weren't* there and I came in and saw you with him—"

He cuts off again and I feel him stand up. He moves away from me. I barely hear his, "I'm sorry," before the flashing lights of the club burn my eyes as the door is pushed open.

I get only the barest glimpse of Dylan's silhouette before he's gone and the door slams shut again.

Leaving me alone.

Used and discarded, with his cum still dripping out of me.

I blink and I'm back there. In that *room*. There weren't any windows in that room either. It stank of cigar smoke and male sweat.

And just like now, I was used like a whore and then left on the floor when they were done.

Christ, are you just gonna lay there? Have some dignity, you useless cunt. Get up.

But I'd been too exhausted, ridden too hard for too long.

What a worthless bitch.

They laughed as they closed the door on me.

At least Dylan didn't laugh, but here I am again.

Why did I ever think pursuing Dylan was a good idea when I've fought *so* hard to get my life back after Bryce? Or is this what I think I deserve? To be broken and left alone in a closet.

When I try to climb up to my knees, I can't. I just can't. I collapse back to the tiles, sobbing so hard I wouldn't be able to see even if there was light.

So I don't see when the door opens again.

And I jump out of my skin when the hand touches my shoulder. I scramble backwards. I guess I can move after all. Terror will do that to a girl.

"Hey, hey, it's me."

Light suddenly illuminates the closet and there Dylan is, crouched over me, his phone lit up like a flashlight.

"Jesus." He looks me up and down and his forehead scrunches in remorse. "Come here." He drops the phone and pulls me to him, pressing my face against his chest.

I know my face is a mess and I try to pull away. "No, my mascara—"

"Hush." He pulls me tighter to him.

I don't relax against him.

He left me here.

Just like him. Just like *Bryce*.

And I felt every inch as worthless as I used to.

I try to push away but he folds me tighter to his chest. "I'm so sorry," he whispers, his mouth right against my ear so I can hear the words in spite of the club music outside. "I'm so fucking sorry, Miranda."

For a long minute, he just holds me.

He holds me until I give in and sink against him. Right after I do, I feel the tremor go through his body. Like he was terrified I wouldn't forgive him.

When I finally pull away, I look up at him. "You hurt me," I whisper.

I know he hears me because his eyes widen in horror. I grab his arm and clarify. "Don't you ever leave me like that again. I can't— I don't know what this is, but if we do it, you can't leave me like that after—" I break off, shuddering. "I just can't handle that, okay?"

He nods. "Come on. Let's get out of here."

It's only when my phone buzzes on the tile that I realize it must have fallen out of my bra when we were having sex earlier. I bend over to pick it up and Dylan grabs my hand and bends with me, like he's unwilling to break contact with me.

I check the phone. It's a text from Daniel. *Where you at, bitch?*

Dylan is looking over my shoulder and he can't hold back his disapproving growl.

I jerk my head to look up at him. "He's just a friend, and that's how we talk to each other. No jealous bullshit."

Dylan swallows and then nods.

I text back: *Mr. Tall, Dark & Sexy showed up. Catch you later next week?*

The response is almost immediate. No words, just three eggplant emojis.

I roll my eyes and Dylan snorts as I drop my phone back in the side of my bra.

He picks up his phone and then, his fingers still interlocked with mine, he opens the door and leads me back through the club. I don't bother trying to find Daniel in the flashing lights that pierce the dark every so often. Chandelier is huge and Daniel's not the kind of guy to be in want of dance partners.

Besides, I'm still a bit shaky on my feet. I'm putting on a good front for Dylan but everything tonight was... *intense*, to put it mildly.

I'm glad when we get out of the club and into the quiet cool of the night air, and even happier when, one Uber ride later, Daniel's guiding me up the front steps to my house.

He hesitates after I put my key in the door and flip the lock.

"Can I—? I'd like to come inside."

I bite my bottom lip and give a slow nod as another wave of relief washes over me. He's not running. Maybe... Maybe this thing between us really could be something different?

"Jesus it drives me crazy when you bite your lip like that," he says, reaching behind me to turn the doorknob and shove the door open.

The next thing I know, he's walking me backwards through the foyer.

We only make it to the couch and he's inside me before he's even kicked off his shoes.

"Jesus Christ," he swears, his jaw clenching above me as his head tips back. Dear God, he's the most magnificent man I've ever seen. His five o'clock shadow is dark and it only makes the perfect cut of his jaw more dramatic.

Then he looks back down at me and his bright, blue eyes are full of so much emotion I feel like I'm looking straight down into the heart of him.

"What are you doing to me, Miranda?" he asks, and I see the confusion mixed with wonder on his face as he slides gently, so achingly gently in and out of me. "I'm no good for you but I can't stay away."

I reach up and cup his face. "Don't. Don't stay away."

I might have been questioning everything earlier, but *he came back*. And he's here with me in this moment, sharing all of himself

"I won't," he whispers, leaning down and brushing his lips over mine, inhaling me. "Because apparently I can't."

I lift up to meet his lips and stop his teasing. He kisses me back the way I love best. Devouring me like I'm the single most important thing in his universe.

And this is how I know he's nothing like Bryce Gentry. When I'm with Dylan, instead of feeling worthless, I feel as cherished as if I'm his everything.

My eyes blink open groggily at the shout. I sit up in bed and flip on the bedside lamp.

Just like last time, Dylan's tossing and turning in the bedsheets. He's having another nightmare. My chest squeezes at seeing him in such obvious pain.

"Chloe!" he cries.

My chest cinches again, for less noble reasons. Who is Chloe? She obviously means a lot to him.

"—kill you. I'll–fucking kill you!" The words are somewhat slurred in his sleep but they're clear enough for me to make them out. And I can hear his fury. His murderous rage.

I scramble back off the bed and stumble to my feet as I call out, "Dylan."

His body jerks but he doesn't wake up. "Fucking kill you!"

"Dylan!" I shout. "Wake up!"

When he still doesn't wake up, I reach over and grab my pillow, then lob it at him. "Wake up, Dylan!"

He gives another shout and then shoots up to a sitting position, looking around him in confusion.

Then he sees me standing several feet away from the bed and it's like I can see the blood drain from his face. He jumps out of the bed, the opposite side from me, and backs up until he hits the wall.

"Dylan." My voice is trembling. "Who is Chloe? And what happened to her?"

He reacts like I slapped him.

"You were talking about wanting to kill someone."

I regret the whispered words as soon as they're out of my mouth because it's like I can see him shut down in front of me.

His face goes blank as he reaches down for his pants.

"Stop it!" I run around the bed to him. "Don't fucking do this again. Don't run."

His eyes squeeze shut when I grab his arms and get in his face.

"Talk to me. Please, Dylan." Then I shake my head. "Shit. Or don't. I'm sorry. It's too early to be pressing, probably. We barely know each other and—"

"Don't say that," he cuts in sharply and the next second his hands are on my face and his eyes are searching mine. "Don't you dare say that. I know you, Miranda Rose. I see you. I see the you that you don't let anyone else see and I know that's a fucking privileged."

"Dylan—"

"No, let me finish." He drops his forehead to mine, his eyes closing again briefly as he nuzzles against me. "I know you, Miranda. But I'm terrified for you to know me. I'm terrified you'll be afraid of what you see," he finishes in the barest whisper.

I'm shaking my head before he even finishes, though. "No. *No*, Dylan. I'm not afraid of you. Don't you get that?" The only thing that scares me is how much I need him, especially considering how short a time I've known him. He's a drug I'm quickly becoming addicted to.

But he gives a violent shake of his head and pulls away from me. "That's because you don't know—"

"Then tell me!"

When he turns back to me, there's a haunted look in his eye. And then he nods. "All right. I'll tell you. I'll tell you because I'm not strong enough to stay away but Miranda, you should make me. And soon you'll know why."

I swallow hard, all the sudden not sure if I actually want to know.

But he's determined now, I can see it. There's an almost masochistic gleam in his eye as he sits on the bed and starts to talk. He wants to tell this story to hurt himself and drive me away and I pray that it doesn't.

"First of all, you need to know that my father was a violent man. He regularly beat and raped my mother."

I suck in a sharp breath.

His voice is monotone as he stares at the wall and continues, "I never understood why my mother stayed." His brow scrunches, like even now he's confused. He shakes his head. "And to this day, it's something I'll never forgive her for."

I blink at the raw bitterness in his voice.

"She died of cancer two years ago but I never spoke to her for the last six years of her life. Not even when she got sick."

A chill goes down my spine at how cold his tone is. Is that what he thinks about all abuse victims? He blames them for staying?

Would he blame *me* for the two years I stayed with Bryce? For all the things I let him do to me?

"But if she was the one who was getting abused—"

He shakes his head and looks toward me. "I blame her for not leaving him because she never even *tried* to get my brother and sister out of that house. Especially my sister. Chloe."

Chloe.

Oh God.

He must see that I'm connecting the dots because his jaw clenches and he nods.

"I don't know how many years my father was sexually abusing my sister before I walked in on them one day six years ago."

My hand claps over my mouth.

"What's fucking hilarious is I thought I'd protected her and my brother Darren, by getting them out of the house whenever Dad was pulling his bullshit. I thought I was shielding them from it. When I moved away to the east coast for college, I told myself they'd be fine because Dad had just had a heart attack. He was weak afterwards and Dare and Chloe were in high school, almost out of the house. I told myself they'd be fine, that I'd protected them from the worst of it."

Dylan walks to the window and slams his palms down on the windowsill. "So fucking stupid. Dad recovered in six months. The truth was I just didn't want the responsibility of them anymore. I abandoned my sister to that monster."

Neither of us says anything for a long moment. And I think about what he said in his sleep until finally I ask, voice shaking, "What happened after you found…" Oh God, I can't imagine walking in on *that*. "Did you kill him?"

I wouldn't blame him, but he shakes his head.

"I gave him a beating, but it was more important to get Chloe out of there. She'd been through enough. He had another heart attack a few months later and died so at least the evil fuck is gone now."

"And Chloe? Is she okay? Now, I mean?"

He tells me about moving her to Austin. "She started out going to community college and eventually transferred to UT. Now she's a music therapist and sometimes she publishes poetry in literary magazines."

He looks so proud when he talks about her and I can see she's the only bright light in this terrible story.

"She sounds wonderful. Do you see her often?"

"No," he barks out. Then, slightly gentler though I can see he's still agitated. "I never want her to have to look at me and be reminded of what she left behind here." He drags a hand through his hair. "People say I look exactly like my father."

"Oh Dylan." I move forward and reach out for him, unable to go another moment without touching him.

But he jerks back, looking at me incredulously.

"What's wrong with you? I just told you that my father raped my sister for years!" he shouts. "That I didn't fucking see it. That I didn't fucking save her. And even after that day, knowing what I know. It doesn't stop me from—" He gestures at the bed. "I still want it like—" He breaks off and his mouth goes into a tight line.

"So you like rough sex. I do, too." I toss my hands in the air. "It doesn't mean you're like your father."

"We both know it's more than rough sex." His eyes cut to mine. "I *want* to hurt you. I want to violate you. I want to hurt you the same way I grew up watching him hurt my mother." He turns away again and his back heaves. "The same way he was hurting my baby fucking sister."

"No," I say firmly. "It wasn't your fault, Dylan. Your father was evil. But you aren't him. You got your sister out."

"Years too late!" he shouts again and I can't help flinching back. He sees it and there's remorse in his eyes. But then he hardens himself again. Like he thinks it's good if he scares me away.

Oh Dylan.

He doesn't know it, but I've looked into the face of evil, and he's not it. How many years has he torn himself up about failing to help his sister sooner? Real evil feels no remorse. It has no empathy, or love, or compassion.

Real evil is Bryce Gentry, laughing with his friends after they all fucked me till I bled, leaving me broken on the floor.

Dylan Lennox is not evil.

He told me this story tonight to try to push me away but it's only done the opposite. I see him so much more clearly now. I see the little boy growing up in that horrible, violent household. I think about how scared he must have been but still he tried to be a good big brother, shielding his brother and sister as best he could.

His whole life he grew up in that role—the protector. And then to find out his sister had been hurt so terribly, of course it would feel like failure to him at the deepest level. To him, he'd failed at his most basic job, the one he'd been doing since he was a child.

I wrap my arms around him from behind and though he flinches, he doesn't pull away.

"Miranda—" he starts but I cut him off.

"Shhhhh."

His shoulders slump and I press the side of my face to his spine. He's carried this burden for so long. So many years the guilt has weighed him down. Guilt for someone else's sins.

"Come with me."

I reach around and take his hand. It's limp in mine but when I tug, he follows.

He pauses on the threshold of the bathroom, though.

"Miranda, you should tell me to go."

I just shake my head and pull him into the bathroom with me. I start running the bath and then turn back to him, tugging his shirt up and off over his head. I have to go up on my tiptoes, he's so tall, but I finally get it off.

He watches me silently as I pull his boxer briefs down and then take off my own shirt and underwear.

I don't miss the way his cock stiffens and I raise an eyebrow and just shake my head. I have no idea how he's always so ready to go. I swear his cock defies nature.

But right now isn't about sex. I take his hand and draw him toward the bath. He steps in and sits down. I get in, too, settling down in the tub behind him, his body between my legs in a reverse position of the last time we took a bath together.

I wrap my arms around him from behind and urge him to lay his head back against my breasts. As I turn on the jets, I feel the tension leave his body.

That's right, baby. Give it all up to me.

"Close your eyes," I murmur.

I look over his shoulder and see that he's obeyed. Then I reach for the large plastic cup I keep on the corner lip of the tub and fill it up, then pour the water over his head. It streams down his face and his mouth opens as he gasps in surprise.

"Sorry, should have warned you."

"No," he says. "It's nice."

I dip the cup and pour another steaming waterfall over his head. I swear he relaxes even more against me.

"Are you baptizing me?"

His sleepy question makes me smile. I was just planning to wash his hair but I like his explanation even more.

"Yes. From now on, you're made new." I run my fingers through the damp hair on his chest. "The past can't hurt you anymore," I whisper.

He grabs my hand, interlocking our fingers.

"I meant what I said before." His eyes are still closed but his grip tightens. "I can't stay away. The only way to be rid of me is to tell me to go."

I shake my head even though he can't see it and wrap my legs around his waist from behind, along with the one arm he isn't already holding.

"I'm not letting you go anywhere."

He groans. "Jesus, I want to fuck you again, but I'm so tired."

I laugh. "You always want to fuck me. But I'll be here tomorrow." I kiss the back of his head. "And the day after that." I kiss him again, this time on his neck. "And the day after that." *Kiss*. "And the day after that."

He growls. "You better be."

And then, tired or not, he turns us around in the tub and pulls me on top of him.

CHAPTER TEN

MIRANDA

The past few weeks have been the happiest of my life.

Are people allowed to be this happy?

I don't think so. Which is probably why, every second I'm not busy being happy, I'm absolutely terrified.

I've never thought of myself as an especially superstitious person, but all the sudden I'm obsessively looking for signs and omens.

Like, I find myself running odds all the time. Daniel just broke up with his Domme of three months, so that means my relationship with Dylan has a better chance of working out, right? Because how likely was it that we'd both find our *ones* at the same time?

Which is really bitchy and horrible of me, but there it is.

But I really feel like Dylan is *it*. *The* guy. The one, like I used to always roll my eyes when people talked about.

I swear though, we fit like puzzle pieces. He gives where I need to take and I think I do the same for him.

Both emotionally and physically. I mean physically, holy *shit*. I didn't know this kind of chemistry was even possible. We spent all weekend together after that night at the club. We barely even got out of bed, and when we did, it was mainly just to eat or bathe... which usually just led to more fucking. Sometimes with rough play and forced scenarios, sometimes not.

Last week I texted him letting him know I'd be waiting in a unisex bathroom of a gas station just off the highway at a particular time and, *God*, my face heats just at the thought of it as I walk with Daniel downtown to get sushi for lunch.

"So I take it things are still good with Mr. Tall, Dark and Sexy?" Daniel asks, bumping my shoulder with his as we walk together.

I blush hotter and Daniel laughs. "It's fine. You can talk about him. Jesus, I seriously need to get out of my own head and drama for a while. So regale me!"

I frown sympathetically and reach out to squeeze Daniel's upper arm. "I'm so sorry things didn't work out with Irina, hon."

He shrugs and looks down at the sidewalk. "It's fine. Her life's too busy and I'm too high-maintenance. It's better it ended now instead of getting dragged out."

I want to press more because I can tell he's hurting but I also know from experience that Daniel shies away from opening up about his feelings—at least without getting him shitfaced first. We've had our deepest conversations when he's *just* hovering at the puke-his-guts-up line of drunkeness. Then he always claims he doesn't remember anything we talked about the next day, even though he's slipped up and referenced things from the conversations later.

To say Daniel is a little emotionally stunted is an understatement. I keep hoping he'll find a partner who can reach him where I can't. Obviously I don't want him drinking all the time just to be able to have real conversations about what's going on in his life.

We get to the restaurant and getting seated and ordering distracts me from worrying about him. As soon as we're settled, though, I drop the bomb that's been weighing on me.

"Dylan invited me over to their family estate to meet his brother. The brother who is the only member of his family he currently speaks to, so it's sort of a big deal. He talks about Darren all the time and I know he's really important to him."

"Ooo," Daniel crows, eyebrows up. "Meeting the family. This is getting serious. Are you going to take him back to Ohio for Christmas?"

"Shut up, I'm being serious." I smack him with my cloth napkin and he jerks back, laughing.

"So was I," he says. "Come on, Mira, when was the last time you've been this excited about a guy?"

That question shuts me up and I look down at my hands in my lap. Daniel sits back in his booth seat. "Oh shit. Not since..." He doesn't finish his thought. He doesn't have to. He knows all about my sordid past with Bryce Gentry. The things that were done to me. The things I did. He's the only person who knows all of it.

"Did you tell him yet?"

I shake my head. "How could I? I was going to but then he made this big confession to me the other night and it just..." I trail off and take a deep breath. "It wasn't the kind of thing you could follow up with an, *oh by the way, that guy who fucked you over that one time while you were going through all that horrible shit you just confessed to me? Yeah, he's my ex.*"

I drop my head into my hands. "I just haven't found a way to slip it naturally into conversation."

Daniel just shakes his head. "Mira, this isn't like you. You usually charge head first into difficult shit. Isn't that what you're always telling me? Just talk to my Dommes about my tendencies so we can work through it together?"

"And how's that going for you?" I snap and then immediately feel terrible.

"I'm sorry." My hand shoots out to grab Daniel's across the table and he shrugs it off like it's fine even though I can see that it's not.

"Shit, Daniel, I'm a world class bitch. I'm sorry. I just feel so guilty every day I don't tell him. I know I should confess the real reason I pushed so hard on getting to know him..."

What would Dylan say if I admitted I sought him out and kept pursuing him because of our mutual past connections to Bryce Gentry? Would he ever be able to look at me the same ever again? If he knew just how far I'd debased myself for Bryce, how much of myself I gave away and lost forever because of that man...

I purse my lips, fighting for control of my emotions. "I've just never had anything like me and Dylan before. It's the best I've *ever* felt. About life. About *myself*. But it feels like... I don't know, like my happiness is a house of cards that could come crashing down any second."

"Damn girl, what are they putting in this sake today?" Daniel holds up the small cup he ordered. "You're all poetic and shit, and it's only," he looks at his wrist, where of course there's no watch, and then fumbles in his pocket and pulls out his phone. "And it's only one-thirty on a Thursday afternoon."

I take my cup and clink it with his. This has been our tradition ever since we were broke kids fresh out of college looking for jobs in the big city.

"So you're going to meet the family which means it's getting intense," he sums up, "but you're also keeping secrets from him."

I drop my forehead on the table. "I'm an idiot. I know I'm an idiot. This is all going to blow up in my face isn't it? That's what always happens in the movies."

"So tell him," Daniel says. "Or don't. Who the fuck am I to be giving relationship advice?" He throws up his hands. "It just sounds like you two are getting hella intense hella fast."

"Is that bad?" I ask, lifting my head. "I really, really like him."

Daniel smiles and it softens the hard lines of his handsome face. "I know. It's good seeing you so happy. The whole time you were with that Chad guy—"

"Chet."

"The whole time you were with him you looked like Barbie. Beautiful but like, made of plastic. With a painted-on smile." He points with two fingers. "And dead eyes."

I'm not surprised Daniel saw what no one else could—how unhappy I was with Chet.

"I want you to meet him," I say. "Dylan. I'm meeting his family and I want him to meet mine."

Daniel arches an eyebrow as our sushi arrives. "You're willing to put him through the Daniel test? Already? This really is serious. You haven't brought a guy to meet me that's ever passed."

I smile with a goofy sigh. "That's because you haven't met Dylan yet."

CHAPTER ELEVEN

DYLAN

I frown as I look over the table set up. "Are you sure it's perfect? I want it to be perfect."

Darren laughs as he claps me on the back. "Jesus, calm your shit, big bro. You got catering for a meal for only three people. And it's the best in the city. I'm pretty sure she'll be impressed."

I shrug off his hand and narrow my eyes at him. "Are you taking this seriously? You better be taking this seriously. This girl is important to me. I want the full Darren Lennox charm offensive. No half-assing it today, okay?"

Darren rolls his eyes as he drags out a chair and sits down at the table. He loosely holds up a hand. "I'll be on my best behavior. Scouts honor. Martha won't leave this house until she's fully charmed."

"Miranda!"

He laughs and slaps the table. "This shit is too easy. Lighten up, man."

"Jesus Christ," I swear, shaking my head and heading back to the kitchen to double check the food is perfect. I don't know why I'm so goddamned nervous. Darren is the only one I have left apart from Chloe and I just—

I breathe out before going into the kitchen, stopping myself from pushing through the door. I've been hovering over the catering staff like a bear ever since they got here an hour ago. I'm sure the food is fine. They're professionals.

I just want everything to be perfect.

The past three weeks with Miranda have been... I can't even wrap my head around it. We've spent almost every night together, either at my apartment or her house. I've never had so much sex in my entire life, even when I was a horny kid in my twenties. Rediscovering sex has been, just... and sex with *Miranda*, Jesus—

No words. No fucking words can do it justice.

During the day I'm constantly thinking of her. But even though I'm getting less sleep than usual, somehow I have more energy than I have in years. For the first time in I can't remember when, I'm passionate again about the product line—the designs of the new robotics boards themselves, but also the business side.

Before Miranda, Darren was the best part of my life. He's the one thing I didn't fuck up. I protected him from Dad and though he had some wild days in college at Stanford, Darren's turned out to be a really good guy. In spite of me, really, because there were times *I* was the bad influence before I got my shit together. Fuck but I couldn't be prouder of him.

The echoing doorbell jolts me out of my thoughts.

She's here.

I freeze for a second before jumping into action.

Darren moves to stand up but I'm already jogging into the foyer to the door. I pause before opening it to look back at him. He followed and is standing in the hallway.

"The full Darren charm offensive," I order one last time before taking a deep breath and opening the door.

It's good I took that deep breath because Miranda looks show-stoppingly gorgeous today. And it's not the outfit. She's just wearing a modest knee length skirt and a white blouse. But Miranda, I swear she fucking radiates.

Her smile is so bright when she sees me that it's like the damn sun coming out.

I lean forward and brush a kiss across her cheek. Even the brief contact is enough to stir my blood. I swallow a groan. My dick's gotten used to seeing her and automatically fucking her.

It's Pavlovian at this point. Seeing Miranda equates clothes immediately coming off, followed by me burying my cock as deep inside her as possible. It's like the first thing I have to do after even the shortest time apart is to reassure myself that she's real and that she's mine. By completely dominating her body. Repeatedly, if possible.

I move back but grab her hand, hoping my dick will get the message that this is just a social call. I don't need to be popping wood in front of my brother for Christ's sake.

I usher her into the house. "Miranda, this is my brother Darren. Darren, Miranda."

She walks forward with a sunny smile, her hand out.

Darren forgoes the hand and hugs her.

"Dylan won't stop going on about you," Darren pulls back with a charismatic smile, "I swear I feel like I already know you."

Miranda's smile goes shy and she glances my way, but I can tell she's pleased by the warm reception.

"Come in, come in," Darren places a hand to the small of her back and guides her to the large, open dining room off the entry way. "We busted out the fancy china and silverware and everything."

Miranda laughs as Darren leads her and pulls out her chair.

I can't take my eyes off her as her eyes dart all around the room. What is she seeing? I spent a big part of my life hating this place. I didn't come back here for years after I found Chloe like that...

It was only after Mom and Dad were both gone and Darren wanted to move in that I could cross the threshold again. Dare did the lion's share of sorting and getting rid of Mom and Dad's stuff. As guilty as I felt about not helping him with it, I just couldn't. No, it was only after he renovated and redecorated that I could step foot back in this house.

And even with the new coat of paint and the wall between the old game room and the living room ripped out to open up the space downstairs, I'm still far too aware of all that went on underneath this roof.

A big part of me still wishes I'd gone with my gut and burned the whole thing to the ground.

But to Dare, I know being able to live on the family estate means something. He seemed surprised when I didn't want to fight him over the deed after dad died. But I just sold him my half at a steal. I used the money to pay for Chloe's tuition and came over here as little as possible.

Darren proposed meeting Miranda here, though, and I knew there was no reasonable excuse to get out of it. And having my thoughts on her all afternoon has kept me from getting stuck in my usual brooding funk that being here brings on.

"So, Miranda," Darren says once we're all seated, "tell me everything about yourself. Then I promise I'll share all the embarrassing childhood stories I have on Dylan."

My chest loosens as I relax, watching the two of them interact. Miranda is lovely as she talks about Ohio and the small town where she grew up, and I only have to threaten Darren with disownment a couple times as he relates some of the more embarrassing mishaps of my early years.

"No way." Miranda's sparkling eyes come my direction. "Where'd you get the cow?"

"Don't believe anything he tells you. *He* was the one who put the cow in the Principal's office on the last day of my senior year. He just *blamed* it on me."

Miranda's head swings back to Darren. "Is that true?"

He shrugs and then smiles slyly. "I plead the fifth."

The food is delicious and Darren keeps conversation flowing. It's always been his talent, far more than mine. In any social situation, he always knows exactly what to say and how to act. Having him as the face of the company was a large part of why we were able to grow as fast as we did. With his marketing and networking skills and my technical and engineering background, we were a force to be reckoned with.

But I've never appreciated him more than in this moment.

Getting to see the two people I care most in the world getting along so well? It means a helluva lot. I catch his eye as the caterers switch out our dinner plates for dessert and give him a small, meaningful nod that I hope lets him see my appreciation.

My phone rings right as I'm about to take a bite of my crème brûlée and I excuse myself from the table.

"Hello?"

"Mr. Lennox. It's Malik here." Malik is my chief software engineer. "We're having a problem with the RISC chips we're testing. The precision of the localization code is *way* off and we're scrambling to figure out a way to fix it."

"Shit." I glance back over to Miranda and Darren, both of whom are looking my way. "I need to finish up with something but I'll be there as soon as I can."

"Okay. As soon as possible would be best. We'll keep working on it, but you've got the most experience with the new chips and everything's stalled out till we fix this."

I give a sharp nod then realize he can't see me. "Got it. I'll text you when I have an ETA."

"What is it?" Miranda asks. "Is something the matter?"

"Just a problem in engineering. I'll need to run over there later this afternoon."

"What happened?" Darren gives me a concerned look.

"Nothing we can't fix. Just a bug with one of the processor's chips we're testing."

Darren shoots me a look. "How many bugs is it going to take before you admit it's a bad idea taking a chance on those new chips?"

Of course he'd use this as an opportunity to take a dig at the RISC chips. He knows we were running another set of experiments with them this weekend. It's true we've been running into bug after bug, but they're all stupid ones. Little things that are easily fixed. The design of the new chips still makes them the best way to go, I'm more and more convinced the more I work with them.

"RISC is the future of robotics, Dare, how many times do I have to tell you? The old processors are shit in comparison. They won't be able to compete—"

Then I glance Miranda's way. Fuck. I'm just putting my foot in it. Her company, ProDynamics, *makes* one of the old Intel-style processors. And I haven't even officially declined the ProDynamics bid. Unofficially, I know I want to go with the RISC chips but we have to make sure they'll work with the rest of our infrastructure first. "I didn't mean—"

"Dylan," Miranda cuts me off, taking her napkin from her lap and putting it on the table. "It sounds like you need to go now. It's okay. Go." Her eyes are earnest and she doesn't look offended in the least about my off-handed putdown of companies like the one she works for. "We're almost done here anyway. I've had a lovely lunch."

Damn, is this woman even real? I pause, wavering. I never want her to think that I consider my work more important than her. And she doesn't even seem upset about her company losing the bid.

She rolls her eyes at me like she can see what I'm thinking. "Dylan, I've seen you almost every day this week, I can handle an afternoon without you."

She stands up to come around the table and I meet her halfway. I cup her face in my hands and give her a kiss. If Darren weren't here it would last much longer but I try to keep it PG. Mostly.

I pull back and search her eyes. "I'll see you tonight?"

She bites her lip. Jesus, it drives me crazy when she bites her lip like that and she knows it. "I'll see you tonight," she whispers, running a hand down my shirt.

Darren clears his throat and we spring apart. Shit. For a second I forgot he was here. Being with Miranda can do that—shut out everything else in the world besides us.

I grin sheepishly at my brother.

"I'll show Miranda out after we finish dessert." He looks to Miranda. "Sound good?"

Her eyes flick my way but then she smiles back at Darren and nods. "Sounds great."

I give her one last kiss and then, with the hand that Darren can't see, I pinch her ass. She stifles a yelp and I grin. "See you tonight, babe."

CHAPTER TWELVE

MIRANDA

Darren and I eat our crème brûlée in companionable silence after Dylan walks out the door. Meeting Darren has been a nice surprise.

I was so nervous all the way over here. What if Darren didn't like me? I know how important he is to Dylan, being the only family that he has left that he's close with.

But things have gone so well that all the nerves in my stomach have finally settled.

After the last bite, I settle my spoon back in the empty bowl and smile Darren's way. "Well this really was lovely. It's been great getting to know the little brother Dylan talks about so much."

"Oh?" Darren asks, eyebrows going up. "He talks about me? That's funny because I was lying earlier. Before today, he's hardly ever brought you up."

I frown. "I'm sorry?" I must have heard him wrong.

"Nothing to be sorry for. I'm just saying that Dylan never talks about his whores much."

My jaw literally drops open. Did he just—? It's several long seconds before I shut my mouth with a clack of teeth.

I shove my chair back. So Dylan's brother is a total jackass. Okay. Well, I'm getting the hell out of here.

But Darren stands up right when I do. And as I skirt the table and head for the door, he grabs my upper arm in a grip so crushing I cry out.

"Where you headed in such a hurry, whore?"

I yank to get away but it's no use, his hold is like iron. "Let go of me," I spit. "Or I'll scream."

He just grins cruelly. "All the catering staff left before Dylan did. No one will hear you. Besides, I thought you liked it rough."

Fear makes all my arm hair stand on ends and my stomach upend. Did Dylan tell him about...? Is that why he thinks this is okay?

Darren wraps an arm around my back like an iron bar and yanks me against his chest. He's hard. I can feel him against my leg.

I scream. Or try to.

But the next second, his big hand is covering my mouth and he's shoving me against the nearby wall. My head bangs painfully against the brick and he's all but smothering me, his hand is cutting off most of the air to my nose as well.

No. *No.* This isn't happening. It's a nightmare.

Wake up. Wake UP, Miranda!

"Oh yeah, you like it rough, don't you, little slut?" Darren breathes into my ear. "But then I've experienced it first hand, haven't I? I've already had your mouth around my cock."

What—?

Tears squeeze out of my eyes as I fight against his grasp. He just shoves me harder into the wall.

Not like Dylan does. With Dylan, it's just enough so that you feel his leashed strength. But Darren pounds my skull into the wall repeatedly until I'm lightheaded. I fight but it doesn't matter. He's huge and his grip is bruising.

"Bryce always told me how well he'd broken his slut."

I freeze at my ex's name. No. Oh God, *no*. Please, no, don't let—

"But I wanted to see it for myself. Lucky for me, Bryce never minded sharing."

No, no, no. I whimper into Darren's hand but he just keeps talking.

"Remember the night Bryce had you in the leather hood and on your knees? When there was a room full of Bryce's friends?"

No. *No*.

"I was one of them. I was there."

My body sags in his grip. I can't help it. Oh *God*.

Darren laughs at my response. "Your boyfriend passed you around like you were a common whore that night. I liked it best when he ordered you to suck my cock while another man fucked you like you were a dog."

"Bryce said we could do whatever we wanted as long as we didn't leave marks. Do you remember that? Do you remember how eagerly you licked and slurped at my cock? I shoved it down your throat so far you gagged. But you still. Just. Kept. Sucking. You were such an obedient little slut."

He laughs and I want to throw up. He was there that night. He— And I— I'm going to throw up.

He laughs even harder as he watches my face. But then all the laughter dies from his features as he leans in and licks my cheek. I wrench my face away but he just grips me tighter.

"I'm feeling in the mood for a repeat, whore. On your knees."

My eyes shoot open wide. No way in fucking hell am I—

His hand comes off my mouth as he starts to unbuckle his pants.

"Fuck you!" I shout at the top of my lungs. "You stick anything in my mouth and I'll bite it fucking off."

Black fury enters his eyes and that's all the warning I get before his fist swings. He lands it in my gut and I double over, wheezing at the pain.

I want to scream for help but he's just knocked all the air out of me. I gasp as he shoves me to the floor.

I scramble away from him and he doesn't immediately come after me. Only because he knows he doesn't have to. There's no way I'll make it to the door before he catches me again.

Shit. *Shit*. How do I get out of here in one piece?

When he takes a step toward me, I hold up a hand and wheeze, "Don't. Don't, or I'll tell Dylan."

Darren just laughs. "Who do you think he'll believe? His baby brother? Or the lying whore he's only been fucking for a few weeks? Especially when he finds out you used to date the man who almost ruined him. Bryce tried to burn his life down."

I shake my head in disbelief as it all clicks into place. "And you let him."

Darren shrugs nonchalantly. "Without dearest big bro in the picture, the company is all mine. Dylan's useful but he's not necessary. And his ethics can be tiresome at times."

I can only stare at him. "You're the monster he's terrified his father turned him into. But it's not him. It's you."

Darren tuts. "It's true that Dad saw quickly enough that Dylan was weak. So he turned his attentions to training me to be the man Dylan never could be."

"An abusive asshole, you mean."

Darren's eyes narrow and he crosses the distance between us in two strides. Then, before I can even get a handle on what's happening, he has me up off the floor and shoved against the wall by my throat.

"I'd be careful how you speak to me, bitch." Spittle sprays on my face as he speaks and I shut my eyes and wrench my head to the side.

He just keeps talking. "Now that I have your attention. Convince him to accept the contract with your company. The old processors worked just fucking fine."

My eyes shoot open at that. Of all the things I expected him to say, *that* wasn't one of them. This is about their *product line*? But no, looking into his cruel eyes, I can see it's about far more than that. He was willing to ruin his brother years ago. He probably doesn't give a shit about which processor they use in their robotics line, he just hates the fact that Dylan had an opinion and overrode him.

And now, if I do what he says— "Dylan might think the only reason I wanted to be with him in the first place was to try to talk him into making a deal with ProDynamics. No, I can't. I *won't*—"

Darren socks me in the stomach again and I cry out uselessly at the pain even as I realize what he's doing—hitting me where it won't leave obvious marks. Just like his father taught him, no doubt.

"If you don't, this gets leaked to Buzzfeed, bitch."

Darren yanks his phone out of his pocket, pushes play on a video, and shoves it in front of my face.

You like that? Dylan growls on the video. It's dark but I can still make him out, bent over me on my Corvette in the garage from that very first night. *You like it when I fucking defile you?*

The video is so clear I can see his hand as it drops to plunge a finger into my backside.

I can't help the cry that escapes my throat as I look back to Darren. How did he even get this footage? It's not grainy like it would be if it were from a security camera. It's color, even.

He just smirks at my confusion. "I hoped throwing the two of you together that night might spark something. But you both performed beyond my wildest expectations."

"How did you—" I wheeze, my eyes shooting back to the video. The angle, and how clear you can see Dylan's face. Then I get it. "You had someone following your own brother?"

"For about a year now," Darren says. "And this was the first time the Golden Boy slipped up. Then again, Bryce did create you to be the perfect victim." Darren rubs a thumb over my bottom lip and I jerk back.

But he's not done. "Not even my brother could withstand you. Not back then and not now. Because oh, did I forget to tell you? At Bryce's party, that time while I was fucking your face? Dylan was the one fucking you from behind at the same time."

His words do what all the blows in the world couldn't.

I go limp. Darren sees it and smiles bigger than he has all afternoon.

He pulls back and shoves me to the floor again. I crumple to the ground.

Of course I always knew it was a possibility. Most of the time when Bryce invited his friends over and passed me around, he didn't bother blindfolding me, but there were a few nights like the one Darren is talking about where he did.

And Dylan was there. Dylan was there the night when... the night when—

I shut my eyes, refusing to think about it any more right now. Because that's exactly what Darren wants and I refuse to give this evil bastard a fucking inch.

Darren looks like he's about to reach down for me again when his phone pings with a text message. Looking annoyed, he glances down at it, then starts tapping out a reply.

He finally puts it back in his pocket and eyes me critically. "Looks like we'll have to finish this another time." He crouches over and gets in my face. "Two weeks. You have two weeks. If Dylan doesn't okay the contract with ProDynamics in two weeks, then I release the video and ruin him so he no longer has a say in the company's dealings. One way or another, I'll get my contract, do you understand, whore? You decide how."

He stands up, towering over me. "You can let yourself out."

And then, because it's what bullies do, he kicks me while I'm down one last time for good measure before he chuckles and walks out of the house.

CHAPTER THIRTEEN

MIRANDA

I get to my feet as soon as humanly possible after he leaves but my legs are wobbly. In part from shock at everything that just happened and partially because I hurt. Everywhere. Darren might have only punched and kicked me in my stomach, but crashing to the ground several times has left me feeling bruised everywhere.

Bruised inside and out.

I stumble out to my car and lock the doors as soon as I'm inside. That's not enough, though, and I pull out of the parking lot, only feeling like I can really breathe again once I'm on the highway speeding away.

Everything I'm feeling... it's so... *familiar*.

I know this.

I lived this for years.

Bryce rarely actually hit me like Darren just did. Maybe that's how I was able to justify living with him for as long as I did? But what he reduced me to was exactly the same as the woman on the floor back there.

When I finally pull into my driveway, the sun has already set, early since it's winter, and it's dark out. I drop my forehead to the steering wheel, then bang it a few times.

Finally I manage to drag myself inside where I immediately start the shower, turning it to the hottest I can possibly stand.

I shed my clothes and stand under the spray.

But the memories are as relentless as the blasting water beating down on my head.

Then again, Bryce did create you to be the perfect victim.

I was an up and coming executive at a tech company when I met Bryce. His fledgling startup, GentryTech was rival to the company I worked for at the time, though mine was much more established.

I was impressed by Bryce but not as in awe of him like so many were.

He seemed to take that as a challenge.

He wanted me. Doted on me. When I finally said yes to going on a date with him, he'd been at it for six months.

He punished me for it later, making him wait like that. And he took great satisfaction in the punishments.

It started small. A word of rebuke or an insult here or there. Often after sex when I was at my most vulnerable.

For all the confidence I projected to the outside world, I'd been a late bloomer and had only had one serious boyfriend before Bryce. And that had been back in Ohio where the boys were, well... *boys* in comparison to the men I'd suddenly found myself surrounded by in the big city. And no one I'd ever met before had anything on Bryce Gentry, who was something altogether different.

The first time he slapped me, it immediately turned into sex, and our sex had always been on the rough side. In the end, was a slap really all that different from a spanking? It was just another facet of the world of kink Bryce was teaching me about, I told myself. It wasn't like he was *hitting me*, hitting me.

But the sex just kept getting rougher and rougher.

Until I knew he was hurting me on purpose. But always, at least in the beginning, he'd make me cum after he hurt me. So often and so regularly that the two became inextricably linked.

Just like he wanted.

It was all so confusing. Only a year before, if I saw a woman like the one he was turning me into on the street, I would have shouted at her to *leave* him! It would have seemed so obvious if I was looking at it from the outside. But Bryce had a way of narrowing down your world until he was all you could see.

All my friends fell by the wayside. Along with my family back in Ohio. Bryce made sure he was my only lifeline.

It was only after I'd burned all my other bridges, after he'd taken over the company I worked for and I was completely isolated and dependent on him that he really showed his true colors.

But it was too late by then.

At that point, he controlled every aspect of my life.

I woke up one morning, bruised and aching, my throat sore from Bryce choking me the night before, wondering how the hell I'd gotten to this point.

I wasn't *this* person. This woman. I wasn't the abused woman who *stayed*.

But I'd let my apartment lease lapse months ago since I was living with Bryce. He was effectively my boss. I barely had any money in savings and there was nowhere else for me to go. I was homeless, worthless, *nothing* apart from Bryce.

Plus, and this was the most disgusting thing of all...

I loved him.

Most days I justified all of it. It wasn't *really* abuse. There were no black eyes. And yes, I hated it when he started 'lending' me out to his friends, but he was always in the room and he said it turned him on to watch me with other men. And that was something couples did, right? Had open relationships?

And if I hated it so much, then why did I cum all the time? Some part of me obviously liked it.

Even if it grew harder and harder to bear. Even if Bryce stopped keeping up with any appearance of caring about me. He ordered me to fuck his friends and then laughed with them about what a whore I was.

But by then I believed every word he uttered so deep down to my center. I *was* a whore. I *was* worthless. I proved it every time I let him lend me out to be used like a hooker and didn't leave the next day. Hookers didn't *cum* when they fucked for money.

But I did.

Because I was a disgusting worthless slut who deserved everything Bryce did to me.

But then there was *that night*. It was the first time there'd ever been so many men at once.

I switch the shower to a tub and then sink down as the water fills. I cover my eyes like I can scrub out the memories.

It's useless, though. That night is seared so deep in my memory it might as well be branded on my soul.

"Christ, you're fat today," Bryce frowned like he was disgusted after he'd ripped my work blouse open and looked me critically up and down.

I'd just asked him what he wanted for dinner and I froze, my eyes immediately dropping to look down at myself. I thought I'd been losing *weight, I'd been so stressed out lately. Nothing I ever did seemed to please him.*

I was fucking pathetic, but all I wanted to do was to please him. I wanted it to be like it had been at the beginning when he doted on me. When he'd been chasing me like I was an exotic creature he couldn't wait to catch and cherish. Where was that man? Had he ever been real at all? Surely he was still there underneath, right?

Bryce had just been stressed out at work. There was so much going on as he strived endlessly to build up Gentry Tech. He was brilliant and would be a billionaire by the time he was thirty. And I got to be a part of it. Behind every great man stood a great woman. That's what they said, right? I was privileged to be that woman for Bryce. So I could stand a few mood swings now and then.

"I'll just have a salad, then," I said. "But I can cook the pork chops I got yesterday for you and—"

"I don't want your fucking pork chops. You can't cook for shit. I'll just order in. You go clean all that shit off your face. We're having guests tonight. Important ones so you better be on your best behavior, do you hear me?"

His tone was so sharp I had to bite back the tears that threatened.

But like always, he could read me. I was an open book to him, no matter how much I might hate the fact.

"Oh, poor baby," he said, his voice gentling. He pulled me in close and ran a

hand down my back. "Shh. It'll all be all right. You're mine and I always take care of what's mine, don't I?"

He pulled back and his eyes searched mine. "Don't I, baby?"

I nodded, swallowing and he smiled.

He had a gorgeous smile and when he gave it to you, you felt like nothing in the world could be wrong.

"Now go clean up." He smacked my ass and I went up to shower.

By the time I got out of the shower, his 'friends' were there.

Bryce's eyes were hard and calculating as he looked me up and down. Gone was the man who'd smiled at me so gently earlier. Sometimes I thought for sure he must have multiple personalities. He could flip like a switch and some mornings I woke up terrified of who I'd find in the bed beside me—Jekyll or Hyde.

It wasn't until much later that I'd realize that no, there was only Bryce, singular, and he merely found it convenient to adopt different masks depending on which was most useful for manipulating his current target.

But I was still his personal toy back then, unwilling to admit to myself the mouse trap I was caught in.

Bryce was waiting for me when I got out of the shower. He didn't let me dry my hair or put on any clothes.

He just put a leather BDSM hood on my head. It had holes for the nose and mouth but that was it. I was blind and everything was muted by the leather. It was disorienting.

Still, I could hear enough to make out Bryce's voice as he ordered, "You accept everything that's given to you tonight, do you hear me? If you don't, I'll be very disappointed and will have to punish you."

I shuddered, both at the words and at his icy tone. I'd disappointed him once before. He'd locked me in a closet for 48 hours with only a jug of water and a bucket to pee in.

He led me down the hallway to the rec room. As soon as we entered, I could smell the mix of competing colognes. The soft chatter of voices stopped as soon as Bryce paraded me into the middle of the room.

Just how many men *were* there?

"On your knees," Bryce ordered me. Then, to the room. "Now, who wants to fuck my girlfriend first? Her mouth or cunt, you can have one or both. She's everyone's whore tonight."

My body went tight and I wanted to yank away from him. He felt me flex and his grip around my arm clenched tighter.

He bent over and hissed in my ear. "Don't you dare fucking embarrass me. There are men here whose business I need. Are you going to help my career advance or are you going to break my promises to my guests and cost me my business? These are lucrative contracts I need."

How dare he put me in this position? my mind screamed. While another part of me whispered: he needs you. You're vital to his business. You can get through one night of this.

"And you know it turns me on seeing you with other men," he whispered, voice going softer for just a moment, his hand caressing down my back. "You'll be safe. They'll all wear condoms. I'll fuck you so sweet after they leave. Do this for us, baby. We're in this together, aren't we?"

Young, dumb, and so fucking naïve, I nodded.

The next moment, there was a cock pressing against my lips. It wasn't Bryce's. It was bigger, for one.

And whoever it was attached to wasn't shy about shoving it down my throat. I choked on it at the same time as a hand reached between my legs from behind. The fingers were rough as they probed me but Bryce had trained my body to respond to rough over the past eight months and almost immediately, I grew wet.

The hand sped up its ministrations the wetter I grew and no matter how brutally I was being face-fucked, I came, choking and spitting up around the cock in my mouth at the same time.

The next moment, the man from behind pushed his cock into me and I was being fucked from both ends. Cheers came from all sides and I began to realize what a herculean task lay in front of me. All these men wanted to fuck me? In one night?

But then someone was playing with my ass as the man continued fucking me. I didn't know if it was the man himself or someone else. Because they weren't all just standing back now. Hands grabbed me from all sides. Squeezing my breasts. Slapping my ass. Slapping my face. Sticking fingers in my ass. Pinching my nose until I really choked for breath on the cock in my mouth.

The man fucking me grabbed my hips and came at me harder and harder with every in stroke, almost rivaling Gentry in brutality. He slapped my ass hard with every outstroke.

Hating myself didn't stop my pleasure from ramping higher and higher again the harder he fucked me.

"*Little bitch is about to come again, Dylan,*" *Bryce laughed.* "*Looks like you really do know how to fuck whores the right way.*"

And then Dylan's grunting voice in response. "*You only know you're doing it right if you can make them cry.*"

Dylan. Oh God it *was* Dylan.

How did I forget the name until now? It's true I've tried to block out that entire night, not *remember* details, but still. Or did some sick, subconscious part of me know all along?

But God, now to know that it was his horrible brother fucking my mouth at the same time. I gag and cover my mouth.

I need some mouthwash.

I need a brainwash.

The water of the bath is finally deep enough, I sink down on my back, completely submerged.

You knew it was a possibility Dylan was there. You knew Bryce and Dylan were acquainted around that time.

It was a few months before his sister moved away, now that I think through the timeline based on my research and what he's told me.

I close my eyes. It's nice down here under the water. Sound is muted. Life is muted. I don't have to be who I am.

What if I just never surfaced? If I just stayed down here? Breathed the water into my lungs?

What does dying feel like?

How much would it hurt?

More than living?

I open my eyes and look through the water at the undulating light on the ceiling. My chest is starting to burn from not breathing.

How long did Dylan stay that night?

One man left early. Was it him? I remember Bryce asking the man why he was leaving so soon. I squeeze my eyes shut and try to concentrate. Had Bryce used a name?

Think. *Think.*

The more I concentrate, the more everything I've tried to repress comes bubbling back up.

"Leaving so soon? What, you're just going to take your fuck and run?"

"I'm sorry, I can't— This is too much for me right now."

Bryce's caustic laughter rang through the room, echoed by several other men.

"Wouldn't have thought you were such a pussy. She loves it. Besides, things are just getting fun."

Two other men were fucking me and concentrating on what Bryce was saying seemed important because I kept thinking: any second he'll call it off. He'll see how hard this is for me and he'll put a stop to it.

"Whatever, man," the stranger said dismissively. Then, "You coming, bro?"

Another voice said no, he wanted to stay. Then there was the sound of a closing door.

It *was* Dylan. I thought when he'd said 'bro' he'd just meant friend. But he'd actually meant *brother*. Because it was Dylan and he was asking if Darren wanted to leave with him.

But of course psycho Darren said no.

I jolt up out of the water, heaving for breath. Water sloshes all around me from the sudden movement and I push hair back out of my eyes.

Dylan wasn't there when things turned so awful later on.

He wasn't there when I begged Bryce to stop. Over and over I cried that I wanted to stop but Bryce just kept ordering man after man to use me however they wanted.

There were no such things as safe words with Bryce.

There was only what he wanted.

I'd trusted him before that night to never let it go too far.

Was Darren one of the men who slapped me so hard that for the first time, I did have a black eye? Was he one of the men who kept on fucking me long after I had no more strength to be up on my knees or to try to fight them off? It must have been little better than fucking a corpse but maybe that was how they liked it.

It went on all night. For hours and hours and hours. Just when I thought it was done, another would enter me.

No matter how sore or bloody or broken I was.

When it was over, when it was *finally* over, Bryce just left me there, in that horrible room.

I thought he'd come back for me after he showed all his 'friends' to the door and help me to the bath. Back in the beginning, after he use me roughly, he used to do that. Take care of me. During the worst times, it was the only thing that made it even bearable.

But Bryce didn't come for me that day.

I don't know how long I laid there on the rough carpet, spent condoms littering the floor all around me.

Hours. Maybe a whole day? I passed out at one point. Not sure I would call it sleep. When I finally got up, the apartment was dark. Bryce was out.

And to my everlasting shame, I didn't leave right then.

The only thing I had strength for was a bath and then to fall into bed, where I stayed for a week.

Bryce only bothered me when he wanted to fuck me. I just laid there and took it, no matter what he did to me.

"Jesus, I guess that finally broke you." He laughed as he said it, the whole time still fucking me. "I was wondering what it'd take. Well, if you don't want to get kicked out on the fucking street you better get some life back in you cause you're fucking boring like this."

He pulled out and left the room.

I finally crawled out of bed and made my way to the bathroom.

I poured the contents of a bottle of some prescription sleeping pills into my hands.

I poured a glass of water.

I dropped my head back and shoved all the pills in my mouth.

... and then I dropped to my knees in front of the toilet and spit them all out, every last one of them.

I flushed and went to the sink to scrub at my tongue.

And then I pulled on a robe and left Bryce's apartment. I didn't take anything other than my phone. I didn't even change or put on any other clothes.

Bryce was wrong.

I wasn't broken completely.

But I was close.

So *very* fucking close.

If I didn't leave then, right that very second, I wasn't sure I'd have the guts to later. So I walked out in my robe.

I dialed the number of an old friend from college. The fact that Paula even picked up the call after I'd completely ghosted her months earlier speaks to what a good person she is.

When I broke down and confessed my situation through tears, she came and picked me up. She let me stay at her place for the weeks it took to find another job and start piecing my life back together.

Bryce didn't have the influence he would have a couple of years later, so he wasn't able to blacklist me like I'm sure he wanted. I was able to find another good job.

I tried to have normal relationships. But it turned out after Bryce, I couldn't cum without pain. I tried. God knows I tried. With a couple of very sweet and earnest men, I tried so hard.

When that didn't work, I looked in other places. BDSM clubs. There I could find men who would hurt me and please me at the same time.

I sought out Jackson Vale, who Gentry had also wronged so badly. I thought we could heal each other. For a while I think it even worked.

But Jackson never genuinely wanted to hurt me. He humored me with light spankings but he never would touch the whip.

Even other Doms I played with throughout the years... there was always something missing. A couple of them genuinely enjoyed inflicting pain but it was always so controlled.

Where was the menace? The manipulation? The mindfuck?

Was that why I really sought Dylan out? Because I hoped he'd be more like Bryce? No matter the research I'd done on him, had I deep down hoped he'd hurt me just like Bryce used to? That he'd tear me down day by day and try to break me?

"What the fuck is wrong with you?" I whisper as I grab the soap and start to scrub at my body.

God, am I so desperate for sensation, to feel fucking *anything* that I was hoping to find Bryce 2.0 in Dylan?

But I didn't. Dylan is the antithesis of Bryce. He doesn't *want* to hurt me.

I stop scrubbing as I stare at the wall.

Because that's not true, is it? Dylan *does* want it. He just hates that he does. He fights against it.

But does that really matter at the end of the day?

Over and over I've told Dylan that it *does* matter. That it's okay to want it because he never steps a toe past the line.

But you've never given him a line.

Really, we've never even come close. All we've ever done is play. Fucking *play*.

I throw the bar of soap in the water and pull the plug, standing up angrily and grabbing for a towel.

I'm done playing it safe.

CHAPTER FOURTEEN

DYLAN

I scrub my hand down my face and sit back in my chair after hours of staring at my damn computer screen coding to fix the bug that had halted testing.

We knew the transition from the old processors to the new might create some kinks in the systems but even I thought we were fucked for a couple of hours there. I was finally able to do some creative rewriting of the code to fix it. In the end it was a matter of reordering some of the divides to maintain precision.

Now we're back on track, with minimal loss of efficiency. But still, this is the fourth bug in as many days and we need to make a decision on which bid to go with soon. We have to be able to prove the RISC chips are a reliable choice *now*, this week, if we're going to stay on deadline.

I'm just about to go for some more coffee when my phone buzzes.

I smile when I see it's a text from Miranda.

Then I read it and my entire body goes stiff. Including my cock.

I'm in the alley outside your building. Come find me.

I immediately press the intercom button on my desk phone. "Malik, you take it from here. I'll check back in tomorrow morning."

"Yes, sir."

Malik sounds surprised. Usually I wouldn't leave when we're under pressure like this, but we've already coded the workaround for this bug and there's nothing to do unless something else crops up. And I suddenly have a can't-miss meeting in the back alley.

I hang up and grab my coat and am at the elevator in a minute flat.

The elevator takes about ten million fucking years getting to the ground floor but finally I'm jogging around the side of the building.

It's chilly and has been dark for hours so there's no one else around, especially since it's the weekend.

Our offices are on the outskirts of downtown so there aren't a lot of people walking by, either.

The back alleyway is empty.

Except for her.

Jesus Christ, what is she wearing?

Or should I say, not wearing?

Is it even Miranda? There's a light on the back of the building but it's casting such long shadows, I can't make out any of her features.

There's still plenty I *can* see, though. The woman has on some high as fuck heels and a skirt so short it almost looks like she's barely got anything on.

Her top isn't much better. It's cut so low her tits are all but spilling out and her only concession to the cold is an obnoxious pink fur cape draped over her shoulders.

She's leaning against the back of the building with one of her legs propped up, knee out, and she's smoking a cigarette. I didn't even know she smoked. She couldn't look more like a hooker if she tried.

I'm still not sure it's Miranda as I slowly approach.

Not until she turns her head languorously at the sound of my footsteps on the pavement.

She blows out a long puff of smoke and then throws the cigarette to the ground, stomping on it with the toe of her pointy heel.

She starts in my direction.

"Miranda?" I call out, my brow furrowing. I still can't tell if it's her or just some working girl who decided to take a break in the wrong alleyway.

The way she sways her hips as she heads my way makes it clear she's looking to sell, whether it's Miranda or not.

"Jesus," I whisper, averting my eyes in case it's not Miranda. I only look back when she's closer.

Thank fuck. It *is* Miranda.

I relax. But only for a second. Because she stomps straight up to me and rears back, then slaps me with what feels like as much force as she can muster.

"What the fuck?"

She pulls her arm back like she's going to try it again and I grab her wrist midair.

She struggles in my grasp and swings her other hand but I catch it, too. She hisses and fights like a wildcat in my grasp.

"I don't care if you're some rich bastard and I'm just a whore. You can't just take me any time you want and then throw me away."

I've never envisioned a scenario quite like this but it's hot as fuck and the idea that Miranda has come here to play instantly has me hard as fuck.

I jerk her close to my chest by her wrists and shove my erection against her stomach before whispering in her ear, "Maybe if you didn't dress like such a whore, I wouldn't treat you like one."

Her eyes flare. "Get the fuck off me," she whispers, shoving against my chest.

I only grin at her.

Oh she came here to play all right.

"I don't think you mean that, baby," I say, and then I lift her with one arm around her waist and drag her deeper down the alley way, into the shadows.

"You fucking bastard," she hisses. "Goddamned fucking bastard."

I slap her ass. Hard.

And then I shove her face first up against a huge metal recycling bin that's as big as a dumpster.

"Maybe I'm tired of you giving it up to anybody who'll pay for it." I shove my cock against her ass. "How many men you fucked today?"

She turns her head and laughs in my face. "I don't know. I lost count."

I slam my hand against the metal of the bin. It feels too fucking good to let the leash off the beast.

"That right?" I growl, ripping at my belt and then shoving the tiny scrap of her miniskirt up. When I reach for her panties, though, fucking holy—she's not wearing any.

"You're such a fucking whore you don't even bother with underwear anymore?" I bring my hand down on her ass. Once. Then again.

"You like making it that easy to bend over so anyone can come along and fuck you?"

I spank her again. Every time my hand makes contact and I hear her little cry, *fuck*. She's so beautiful. So fucking perfect. Giving herself like this to me.

I reach between her legs and Jesus Christ, she's fucking drenched.

She wants this just as much as I do.

She always does.

She was made just for me.

I don't bother with any more words. I just shove my cock home. Where it was always meant to be. Stuffed up her pussy to the fucking hilt.

She gasps at the intrusion and her hands scrabble against the metal of the bin.

"This is what you've been begging for, isn't it, slut?"

I yank back and then hammer in again. "You love being pounded with dick. You can't fucking get enough of it, can you? Fucking can you?" I hiss in her ear when she doesn't respond.

"No," she whimpers.

"No, what?"

I grab her by the back of her hair and give her a rough shake.

"No, I can't get enough of it," she gasps.

But right after she says it, she really starts fighting me. I grip her wrists and hold her in place, fucking her mercilessly. But then she starts squirming. Liking it too much.

"Not yet," I growl. "Not fucking yet, whore."

I yank her away from the recycle bin and together, we go down to the ground. That fucking terrible fur cape should protect her back from the asphalt, so at least it's good for something.

Because I don't want to take it easy on her.

No, now that I'm looking at her, I need it.

I need her tears.

I need to fucking make her cry.

She sees it in my eyes and the slightest smile crosses her face, then the next second she's slapping at me again. Fighting my intrusion.

But she doesn't even know intrusive yet.

"You're gonna fucking take it like any little whore should."

I pull out of her pussy and then reach down to reposition myself.

At her other hole.

Her eyes widen and she bites her bottom lip as she feels me there.

Usually I go slow.

Usually I prepare her.

Usually.

But not fucking today.

All week, our lovemaking has been sweet. Gentle caresses in the morning. Needy hands in the shower.

But this is what we both fucking *need*.

So I slam my cock up her asshole with only the juice of her cunt to lubricate the way.

Her entire body jolts and her features scrunch in pain.

I almost cum on the fucking spot.

I pull out and then ram back in again and fuck, oh fuck, there it is.

The first fucking tear.

I lean over and bite at her cheek before tasting it with my tongue. Salt and perfection.

"Let me hear it," I groan as I thrust in for the third time into the impossibly tight grip of her ass.

She whimpers in pain and a shudder works its way down my spine. Again. I need it again. More.

"Give me fucking more," I demand, pistoning out and then in again. "Tell me how much it fucking hurts."

"It hurts," she cries. "It hurts so much." She's weeping now and I cover her with my body, elbows beside her head on the fur.

"How does it hurt? Tell me. How does it hurt?"

"You're splitting me open," she says and then gasps, biting her bottom lip and arching her breasts up into my chest.

Oh fuck, there it is, the pleasure mixed with pain that might be the only thing more beautiful than her tears.

"That's right I'm splitting you open," I say harshly, reaching down to twist her nipple.

She cries out and then buries her face against my neck.

"It hurts," she weeps in my ear. "It hurts so good."

Jesus fuck.

This woman. This goddamned woman.

I thrust my hips, making sure to grind against her right where she needs it. One more thrust and then I feel it—her whole body shakes as she orgasms.

I let her cry it out against my neck as she clenches around my cock, wave after wave of pleasure rippling through her body if the way she's clenching on me is any indication.

It takes everything in me but I hold it back because there's one last fantasy I've never lived out with her and in this moment, it'd be perfect.

I slip out of her ass and then grab her by the back of the hair, kissing her on her forehead as I go.

"On your knees," I whisper. "Now take what I give you like a good girl."

When she doesn't move quick enough, I order more harshly. "On your knees, whore."

Her eyes flash up at me and I give a rough tug on her hair, grabbing her upper arm to help her up onto her knees.

"That's right, on your knees. Now take everything I give you."

I stand over her, feeling like a fucking god.

I keep an iron grip on her hair and start to jerk myself hard, wanting to see my cum splash all over her face.

"Look up at me, slut."

But her eyes are wide and she jerks back. Oh so that's how she wants to play it?

I smile and am about to grab her hair even tighter and jerk her back into place when she says, "Red. Red!" and scrambles back from me, holding up her hands like she's afraid.

Like she's afraid of me.

CHAPTER FIFTEEN

DYLAN

She looks at me like she's afraid.

Afraid.

Of me.

My dick has never shriveled so fast. What the fuck? Have we not been on the same page this whole time? Did I do something—?

"I'm sorry," she mumbles, getting up, wobbly on her skyscraper heels. "I'm sorry. I should never have come here like this."

Then she moves like she's going to try to get around me and leave.

"Miranda. Miranda!" I bark louder when she ignores me. I want to reach out and grab her but draw back at the last minute.

She had to use her safe word.

She had to use her motherfucking *safe word* with me.

I'm bent over before I know it and my lunch plus the shitty chips and soda I ate earlier while I was working all come back up as I vomit against the wall of the building.

"Dylan!"

Miranda's small hand rubs my back and my eyes water as I shake and wipe at my mouth with my forearm.

I stand up and stumble away from the wall. Away from her.

"Did you not want—" I gesture back down at her fur cape several feet back by the recycling bin. "I thought it was another game. Jesus, Miranda, I'm so sorry, I thought—"

"It was," she cries, sobbing even harder now. "I came here wanting—" She breaks off with a fresh round of sobs and it kills me, fucking kills me seeing her like this.

I reach a hand out but she just shakes her head and takes a step backwards. "I'm fucking toxic, can't you see that? You need to stay the fuck away from me."

"What are you talking about? Where is this all coming from?"

Then I look around. I am not having this discussion, whatever the fuck this is, in a cold alleyway behind my fucking building.

I walk toward Miranda and this time when she tries to step back, I don't let her. I put an arm around her shoulder.

"We're going to get in my car and drive home. And then you're going to tell me exactly what the fuck is going on."

She shakes her head and her whole body shudders with her sobs but I don't let up. Something is seriously fucking wrong and I won't rest until I've gotten to the bottom of it.

I only let go of her long enough to shrug out of my jacket and sling it over her shoulders, then I pull her close and walk her as quickly as I can back around the building to my car.

Being the boss, I have a parking spot right up front so we don't have to go too far. I open the passenger side door and get her seated, tucking her legs carefully inside. She's not crying as hard but she's gone oddly listless. Frankly, she's scaring the shit out of me. I tug her seatbelt across her and secure it in place.

I wish we were anywhere but out in public.

I run around the front of my Tesla and hop in the front seat. Then I drive as fast as I dare to my apartment, shooting quick glances over at her the entire way. She has her head turned away from me. I call her name several times but she doesn't respond.

When we finally get to my building, I pull the car into valet and run around to her side. I tug her out of the car and then lift her into my arms. She doesn't fight me, thank Christ. She just sinks against my chest as I hike her up in my arms, one arm under her back, the other under her knees.

I ignore the look that the doorman and a couple in the lobby give us and head straight to the elevator, dipping down with Miranda to hit the button for my floor.

Miranda just keeps her face burrowed into my chest.

Meanwhile I swear my heart is beating a thousand fucking beats per minute. She's hurting and I don't know why... except I do, don't I?

I was the only other person in that alley way. *I* hurt her. But I swear to God I'll make up for it. Somehow, I swear— Jesus, I swear I'll spend my life making up for—

The elevator pings and as soon as the doors open, I sweep out of the elevator, unlock my door with my keycard, and take Miranda straight back to my bedroom where I lay her down on the bed.

She immediately curls onto her side, back to me, her knees up to her chest.

Just watching her sends a sword through my chest.

It's the same position I found Chloe in that day.

For a second I can't breathe. Can't move. Can't fucking do anything.

Monster.

I take a stumbling step back from the bed.

Jesus, what was I thinking, bringing her back here? I hurt her, obviously she wouldn't want to be alone with me.

I take another step back but then she lifts her head off the bed and looks over her shoulder at me.

"Hold me?" she asks, her voice barely a whisper.

My chest clenches in gratitude and relief and lo—

I all but launch myself onto the bed and curl my body in a shell around hers. She starts to cry again and I wrap my arm around her waist. She clutches me, her nails digging into my forearm like she's so terrified I'll disappear, she has to hold on to me for dear life.

I want to ask her what's wrong—no, I want to *demand* it. But I've never seen her so fragile. It's a word I would usually never associate with Miranda Rose. She's usually got that shield of armor that's ten feet thick.

But not with me. Every time we're together, I get to glimpse more and more of her.

And tonight, for one reason or another, her defenses have collapsed completely.

My cock stirs in my jeans but I move my pelvis back from her ass. I don't want her feeling my need, or to know that even now when she's so clearly distraught, I still want to fuck her.

It's the vulnerability and the honest, beautiful core of her that's attracted me from the start. I never needed her beautiful body or her perfect face—it was this, her willingness to crack open and let me connect to this intimate, vulnerable part of her that attracted me the most from the beginning.

I'm not sure she even realizes what a gift it is to a man like me, who kept himself set apart from human emotions for years.

"Do you know how rare and perfect you are?" I whisper.

She turns her head, her mouth dropped open and I can see by her look that she thinks I'm crazy. I can't stop myself from dropping my mouth to hers.

I intend it to be a gentle, reassuring kiss.

But nothing's ever simple when it comes to this woman, is it?

She flips in my arms and grabs my face, devouring my mouth and cementing the front of her body to the front of mine.

She groans into my mouth when she feels my hard-on, thrusting her hips up to grind against it.

I growl and with every ounce of discipline I have left, I pull back from her. "No, Miranda, we don't have to. You were so upset earlier. We can just talk, or hold each oth—"

She cuts off my words with another hungry kiss. And then she reaches down between our bodies and grabs my cock through my jeans. She whispers, voice heavy with need. "Please, Dylan. I need you inside me. Don't make me wait."

Well fuck, if she puts it that way…

Still, the memory of her calling *red* and the look on her face. I breathe out hard and then roll us so that I'm on my back and she's on top.

"Put me inside you if you want me."

Her hands are frantic on my pants, unbuckling and then unbuttoning them. When her hand closes around my cock, I can't help hissing and throwing my head back into the mattress.

I lift up my hips as she yanks my jeans down a little.

And then, fuck, *yes*, she's on top of me, centering me on her hot cunt and lowering herself on my shaft. I can't help grabbing her hips and thrusting up into her as I drag her down until I'm bottoming out inside her. Even with her on top, I still can't give up control.

But she doesn't seem to mind, letting out a mewling noise and thrusting her breasts out, the most magnificent fucking image as she rides me.

I don't know how or why, but everything that seemed complicated or impossible moments ago all fades away the second I'm inside her.

Of course we'll work through this, her body says as it receives mine so eagerly. *You were made for me.*

She lifts off and then rocks back down over me, her breasts jiggling as her body shudders.

My cock hardens and elongates inside her. It's different from earlier in the alley. I'm not playing a part.

Do I still want to hurt her? I look up at the beautiful goddess above me and all I feel is the overwhelming and absolute need to… *protect* her.

All the breath expels from my chest at the realization.

"Lower," I demand. "Get down here."

She immediately lowers herself and I wrap my arms around her back, securing her to me because even though I'm inside her, it's not close enough. Never close enough.

I slow my upstrokes and tangle my other hand in her hair, but only so I can urge her head just the slightest bit back so that her eyes are on mine.

And for the first time in my whole life, silently, I make love.

I never break contact with her eyes as I stroke in and out. She grinds down and rolls her hips in time with each of my thrusts until we're so in sync, I can't tell where I end and she begins.

When her eyes fall closed as her pleasure ramps higher, I shake my head and demand in a soft whisper, "eyes."

Seconds later, tears film her eyes, but not because I'm hurting her. It's because of this beautiful moment we're creating together.

"That's right. Give it to me," I say. "Give it all over to me."

And she does.

Her hands ball in the sheets beside my head and her breasts heave against my chest as her face scrunches in pleasure. But she looks at me the entire time, and the spasm that rocks through her body as her orgasm begins is the most fucking beautiful thing I've ever seen.

Her pussy squeezes around me and she looks lost. So fucking lost in her pleasure, lost in me, lost in her wanting finally being satisfied.

I thrust up deep and I cum too, so deep inside her, so deep.

And even though I've loved watching her cum and sharing it, I can't stand another second without her mouth. I grab the back of her head and drag her mouth down to mine.

I kiss her hard, tasting her sweet mouth as I pull out and push in again, another groan tearing its way out of me as she squeezes the last of my cum from me. She's still shuddering, still riding her high and I roll my groin against her just where she needs it.

I drink in her gasps and breathy whines of pleasure. Her arms fly around my back as she pulls me even closer to her.

"Dylan," she cries as her body continues to shudder as she swivels and rolls her hips on my still hard rod. "*Oh*."

Fuck. She has to be riding a second orgasm at this point and it's so fucking hot.

"*Ohhhhh*," she squeals, back arched, mouth open, holding the position for three seconds, five, shit, I keep grinding upwards, kissing her neck, wanting to give it to her, every ounce of pleasure, until finally she collapses on top of me, obviously spent.

Her forehead is dotted with perspiration and her cheeks are rosy and she's the most glorious fucking thing I've ever seen.

I kiss her rose-red lips, swollen from my kisses.

And I whisper the only truth it feels like I've ever known: "I love you."

CHAPTER SIXTEEN

MIRANDA

I didn't tell Dylan I loved him back last night.

How could I when I'm keeping so many secrets from him?

And of course, him being him, he didn't press me or even look upset when I didn't say it back. He just kissed me and held me tight all night, then woke up early and cooked me breakfast in bed.

I push my chair away from my desk and look out the window. My office isn't huge but I have a good view. I stand up and stretch my legs as I look out on the city.

I'm sore and my eyes close in shame remembering exactly why. What was I thinking going to Dylan's office like that last night?

Was I trying to test him? To see if he was like his brother?

I rub my temples.

Dylan's nothing like Darren. I knew it the second he touched me in the alley. I realized how stupid I was to have ever second-guessed him so then I decided to just be with him, to live out the fantasy like we always did.

But then he ordered me on my knees. Just like his brother had earlier that day.

It was too much, too soon.

Not that Dylan could have known. Not that I had any business being there, doing anything like that when I was still so emotionally fucked up from the afternoon.

And God, the horror on Dylan's face when he thought he'd hurt me.

I've never hated myself more than I did in that moment.

That I could make him think that for a *second*—

I just wanted to run away. To break up with him because I'm toxic. Couldn't he *see* that? The fact that I sought him out at all after what happened with Darren is so fucked up.

And if he ever finds out my connection to Bryce, it will only hurt him. I should never have sought him out in the first place.

And God, if Darren releases that *video*.

I'll ruin him.

One way or another.

I'm going to ruin this beautiful man.

And I was still too selfish to break up with him. I told myself I would when we got back to his apartment. But then he held me and the next second, made such sweet love to me.

Even now, I'm justifying it. Because, after all, Darren might still release the tape even if I did break up with Dylan. He didn't ask me to break up with Dylan. He asked me to get Dylan to reconsider the contract with ProDynamics.

Underneath, I know it's just selfishness. I can't bear to lose him. Not yet. Getting lost in his arms last night was everything I needed. More than I ever expected or ever hoped for myself. I never even knew anything like that kind of passion and connection *existed*.

I love you.

I flop back down in my chair, running his words over in my head for the millionth time. He *loves* me.

But would he still love me if he knew the truth? The whole truth about how I let Bryce whore me out? About how Dylan himself had been one of the men who had used me, along with his own horrible *brother*?

Thoughts of Darren only make my stomach sour. Dylan has no clue that he's in business with a viper. Another secret. But is the only way to protect Dylan really to betray him by pushing him into doing what his brother wants? To lie to him and manipulate him?

If I push it hard enough and make it obvious enough what I'm doing, maybe Dylan will want to break up with *me*. Maybe I can make it look like that was why I pursued him in the first place. All so I could secure the contract for my company.

Maybe he'll get disgusted with me and make the break I can't. Then he'd be free from my taint.

God, even the thought sends my heartbeat racing in terror. A life without Dylan?

I haven't known him long and I might never be able to admit it to him, but God, of course I love him. When you meet the other half of yourself, you're a fool if you don't hold onto them as hard as humanly possible.

Meeting him has been like... like *coming home*. That's the only way I can describe it.

So there's only one way forward.

I can't lose him. No matter what.

I breathe out and reach for my phone and type out a quick text, then hit send before I can second guess myself:

Swamped today but missing you. Think you could come by the office to have lunch with me at my desk?

His response was almost instantaneous: *I'll bring Chinese takeout from that place you love.*

I'm a wreck for the rest of the morning, barely getting anything done other than answering a few emails. Every few seconds, I glance back at the clock. Naturally, it's moving at an agonizingly slow pace.

A couple of weeks ago my boss himself came by my office. He said he'd heard that I was dating a Lennox brother.

"You know bids are still out for their new robotics line. Whoever gets that contract will be secure for the next decade. So maybe you could smooth the way or put in a good word for ProDyn—"

"Absolutely not." I was so vehement and righteous in my indignation. "I do not mix my work and personal life and I won't apologize for it."

"I'm sorry," Rod backpedaled, lifting his hands, "I'm sorry. I didn't mean to try to put you in an awkward position. Forget I said anything."

I heard what he was really saying. Don't mention him trying to pressure me to Dylan. The last thing Rod wanted was a negative impression of ProDynamics making its way back to Dylan either. I just lifted my chin. "Like I said, I keep my work and personal lives completely separate."

He nodded and ducked out of my office without another word and that was that.

And now here I am. It only took a Darren sized wind to swing my moral compass so far from north I hardly recognize myself as I wait for Dylan to arrive.

It's finally half past twelve and I can't stop my toe from tapping nervously on the carpet underneath my desk. It's a terrible nervous habit of mine. Thank God the office is carpet, not tile. With the carpet, no one can hear the tapping, and from the waist up, I can usually manage to look completely composed no matter what's thrown my way.

Of course, the stakes have never been so high.

Right on time, I hear a knock at my office door. I shoot to my feet even as I call out, "Come in."

Dylan pushes open the door with a wide smile, holding the bag of Chinese takeout like a proud delivery boy.

In spite of everything, seeing him brings a genuine smile to my face. I don't know how to describe it exactly, but Dylan's very presence makes me relax. He just exudes this energy of masculine protection that makes me want to kick off my heels and run the few feet to him, then throw myself in his arms.

If only I could confess everything to him.

But God, what would Darren do if I did? Dylan obviously has no clue what kind of man his brother is. For them to have both gotten to this age without Dylan the wiser, Darren must be one slick bastard.

Just the thought sends shivers down my spine.

So I don't throw myself into Dylan's arms. Instead I just smile and gesture at my desk. "Lay out our feast. I'm starving."

Dylan's smile dims for a moment like he senses there's something off with me but he comes over to the desk and starts pulling boxes out of the bag, along with chopsticks.

Okay, here comes the bit of acting I've been prepping for all morning.

I pick up my laptop and move it over to the edge of my desk and then start shuffling the papers I had spread out.

They're blueprints and test output reports of our newest processor with my scribbled handmade notes in the margins of all the papers. Something I did only so it'd seem believable for me to have actual printed out papers on my desk instead of just on my laptop.

But now I'm embarrassed about how blatant my ploy to gain his interest is. And I have to stop myself from cringing when he asks, "What's that you're working on there?"

Shit.

He's taking the bait.

You need this. He *needs this, even if he doesn't know it. Darren will ruin him if you can't convince him to take the deal.*

I continue stacking the papers. "Oh, it's nothing."

He snatches one before I can add it to the stack. "The ProX8 Processor."

"Hey," I grab playfully for the paper. "That's proprietary information."

He rolls his eyes. "I've already seen all the specs when your boss put in his bid a month ago and sent over a prototype for us to test."

"Yeah," I say. "But if you were interested, we would have heard by now. And it's fine, we have other contracts."

I snatch the paper out of his fingers, right as a furrow scrunches his brow.

"You guys put in a bid with Pantheon?" He doesn't even try to hide his disapproval in his voice, referring to the collaboration proposal sheet I just snatched out of his hand. "Their laptops are shit. It'll make your company look bad when their machines malfunction. You'll be tied to them in people's minds."

I shrug. "We know their motherboards don't have the best reputation but they've assured us they've improved quality control in the last few years." When his expression doesn't change, I sigh. "You know how hard it is to get contracts in this day and age. Intel cornered the market and companies like yours are exploring other solutions. We have to take what we can get."

"But this is your central product line you're talking about," Dylan argues.

"It'll be fine. We'll request some further quality control measures as part of the contract."

But Dylan's just shaking his head. Vehemently. "Miranda, I've seen their factories. A lot of our workers in Thailand come from Pantheon factories and the conditions are terrible. They're little more than sweatshops. Their safety standards are shit, they don't treat their workers well, and their products come out half-assed. You can't accept a deal with them."

I frown down at the desk.

This is exactly the reaction I was hoping to get from him but now that I am... Is this how easy it was for Bryce every time he manipulated people? Manipulated *me* until he had me exactly where he wanted me caught up in his spider's web until I thought I had no way out?

Dylan runs his hands through his hair. "I really thought the RISC chips were the way to go but every time I turn around, we run into one problem after another with them. This weekend was just more of the same."

I feel my eyebrows pop up at this.

"Maybe as much as I want them to work, Darren's right, the tech just isn't there and we should try again in a few years with the launch after this one. We're running out of time to start getting our line in production. We have to figure out the processor situation."

Darren.

I frown. Is it really a problem with the RISC chips themselves or is

Darren doing something to sabotage the experiments? Would he do that, just to get his way?

I think of him standing over me in the dining room, that smug, superior smile on his face.

Yes, yes he absolutely would.

But Dylan is still talking.

"And it's not that the ProDynamic processors were bad. I had engineers run tests with every processor that came in with the bids and the Pro processors performed among the best, and the price was right." He sighs. "I just really wanted the RISC chips to work."

He pauses, looking out the window. "But maybe it's time we took another look at—"

"Come on," I cut him off, offering a half-hearted smile, pushing a box of General Tso's his way. "Eat it while it's hot."

I open up my sweet and sour chicken and shove a huge bite in my mouth. I can sense that it's delicious but it tastes like sandpaper. My appetite is completely gone.

"Miranda?" When I look up, Dylan's watching me with a hawklike gaze. I shiver underneath it. "Is something wrong?"

"What?" I try to laugh it off as I choke down my mouthful of food. "Of course not." I shove another large piece of sweet and sour chicken into my mouth.

I can't answer pointed questions with my mouth stuffed, can I?

For a few blissful minutes, it's silent, the both of us eating.

But I can feel Dylan's eyes on me. Does he see my guilt written on my face? In the slump of my shoulders? Written in a scarlet letter across my forehead?

Jesus, I barely had to do a thing. He was talking himself into doing exactly what I wanted. Well, what *Darren* wanted. God, I feel sick. Shoving food down my throat is *not* helping, either.

"Enough," Dylan says, slamming his food down on the desk after several more silent minutes have passed.

"What?" I jump at the sudden action.

He yanks the box of chicken out of my hands and throws it back into the bag, along with his and the other few containers on the desk. Then he stands up and walks around to me.

"What are you—"

He doesn't answer, he simply lifts me up off the chair and bends me over my own desk. He gives my ass a sharp smack before yanking my skirt up.

I gasp at the rough treatment. But at the same time, when he reaches underneath my underwear to probe at my entrance with a finger, I'm already slick with wanting him.

He strokes me up and down between my lips and finally slips his forefinger inside my sex. All the while he strums at my clit with his thumb, and I'm putty in his hands.

I hear the telltale jingle of his buckle unbuckling and then oh God, oh yes, I feel the head of his cock at my entrance.

He bends over my back and then thrusts inside. I bite my lip and groan as I grip the edge of the desk, loving the invasion. Loving him.

In minutes, I'm on the edge. I clench around him as hard as I can, reveling in the feel of his intrusion as he slides in and out.

It's difficult but I muffle my whimpers, biting my own hand to stifle the pleasure that wants to scream out of my throat.

So close. It's right there. I swivel my hips and press back against Dylan with his every thrust. Almost there— Just one more—

Dylan drops his hand around to strum my clit and *oh*— It starts to hit. But then, wha—

Dylan stops.

Everything.

Just.

Stops.

I whimper and look over my shoulder. Dylan's face is serious as the grave.

He leans over and breathes kisses over my temple. My entire body shudders, tremors of the waiting orgasm still teasing me.

"It seems like the only way I can get complete honesty from you is when I have you like this. With my cock buried inside you."

He shifts, pulling out and then shoving to the hilt again and I stifle a groan.

"Now tell me what's wrong and why you clammed up earlier when I was looking at the blueprints. And don't you dare try to lie or hide shit from me."

I can't help the tear that crests and then falls down my cheek.

Of course he could see I was lying. I can't keep anything from him. He'll see through my bullshit every time.

But I *have* to protect him.

That's what love means, no matter the sacrifice to him.

So I tell him as much of the truth as I can.

"If Pro got the contract with Lennox Brothers, it would solve so many problems," I confess, my voice watery. "But I hate the thought, *hate it*," I whisper vehemently, "that you would think I would ever use this relationship to get ahead at work."

I reach back and grab his face. "I swear," I look him in the eyes, "I would never do that. Never use you just so I could get ahead. You're everything to me." I press my forehead to his. "Everything. You're my *everything*."

He pulls back and then surges inside me again. And again and again.

"Jesus fuck, I love you," he whispers harshly before his lips crash down on mine and my orgasm finally crashes over the edge into a blinding white light.

CHAPTER SEVENTEEN

DYLAN

The rain is pouring as I push back into my office after my lunch date with Miranda. Jesus, that woman. She hasn't told me a lot about her past but I'll bulldoze down her barriers one at a time. I swear I will.

In time, she'll learn she can trust me with everything. And while I've never historically been a patient man, with her I can go as slow as she needs.

I close my eyes, savoring the taste of her on my lips. The sweet smell of her. The feel of her body clenching around me.

Then I shake my head and grin. Jesus, I have actual work to get done this afternoon, but later tonight…

I whistle as I head up the elevator.

Later tonight I'll be happy to do some more explorative boundary busting.

The pep in my step must be obvious because Darren is in the lobby chatting with Sylvia, our interim Executive Assistant while Hannah is on vacation to visit her grandkids.

Darren turns my way.

"Are you... *whistling*? What's got you in such a cheerful mood."

I throw out my hands. "It's a beautiful day."

Both Darren and the young blonde woman behind the desk look in confusion to the window where it's gray and the rain is pouring.

I just laugh. "Oh, and there's the fact that I'm in love. That might have a little something to do with it."

Darren's mouth drops open. Literally drops open and I laugh, walking up and shutting it for him. "Watch out, little brother, you'll catch flies like that."

I walk past him, giant smile still stretching my face. "Be in my office in twenty, Dare. I know you're flying out to the manufacturing plant outside Bangkok in a few hours, but we need to call the investors together. I want to make the contract with ProDynamics happen after all."

"What?!"

I hear Darren's footsteps hurrying behind me as I head toward my office. I smile at the shock on Darren's face. "But what about the future of robotics? And being on the cutting edge and all that shit? You've been fighting for RISC for months!"

"What can I say? Between all the trouble we've been having in testing and you wearing me down about it every day, I'm finally listening to reason."

And the idea of Miranda being the liaison for the length of the contract, yes, I like that very much. Everybody wins. We can try the RISC chips in another few years after they've worked out all the bugs and they're more stable.

"That's great news," Darren says as we step into my office, "but are you really saying this didn't have anything to do with a certain brunette beauty that had you scampering off when you never take lunch? She works there, doesn't she?"

Then he pauses. "Oh." Another pause. "I see."

I narrow my eyes at him. "It's not like that. If we aren't going with the RISC chips, there's no reason not to use Pro processors. They tested among the best of the older style. You know, the kind *you've* been nagging me to go with, ad nauseum. I don't get what the problem is."

But Darren doesn't look happy like I thought he would at hearing the news. To tell the truth, he looks grim. "Look, brother," he claps a hand on my shoulder, "I hoped this thing would fizzle out on its own and I'd never have to have this talk with you..."

I shrug his hand off. "What the fuck are you talking about?"

He sighs and runs a hand through his hair.

"I had my guys look into her."

My jaw clenches and I only barely stifle the impulse to shout my next words. "You *what*?"

He holds up his hands. "Look, Dylan, this girl shows up out of nowhere and suddenly it's like you're a different person and now with this contract. I just had to make sure she was legit. So I had some of my guys do some digging and—"

"And nothing." I stand up and get in my brother's face. "You and I know better than anyone how false things can look without context. What if she ran a so-called *search* on me? She'd think I was a... a *rapist*." I almost choke on the last word and I can't believe Darren would pull this shit.

But Darren just stands up taller. "I'd say I'm sorry but I'm not. Dylan, you need to hear what I found out. Did she tell you that she used to date Bryce Gentry?"

"What?" I bark, taking a step back like he slugged me.

"Yeah." Darren's nodding. "They dated for two *years*. She could still be working for him, even while he's in prison. He could be trying to manipulate you into another scandal or—"

"Shut the fuck up," I shout, turning my back on him and pacing away several steps. Miranda dated *Bryce*?

She dated...

My stomach drops to the floor as I remember that day. Before I found Chloe, Bryce was bragging about that night. That night after I left.

"You had fun at our party the other night, didn't you? You missed the best part, though." Bryce smirked. *"It really got rowdy after you left."*

He laughed as he pulled out his phone and pushed play on a video. "Look. We fucking broke the bitch but she loved every second of it." And there was the *woman with the leather hood on, limbs splayed out helplessly as Bryce crouched over her, his foot on her face as he fucked her ass from above.*

Her whole body jerked with the force of every merciless down thrust.

The cameraman walked around them, leaning in especially close so you could hear her pathetic whimpers as she cried.

"She was sobbing by the end, you would have fucking loved it," Bryce laughed. "Oh, wait for it, wait for it—" *he pointed at the screen.*

A high-pitched wail strangled its way from the woman's throat.

"See, the bitch still cums. That slut loves the fucking pain. I taught her to. She's my bitch. It took a couple years but now she can't fucking cum without it."

"Damn," I said, looking at the video, hard as stone and wishing like fuck I'd stayed to the end of the night. "Wish I had a girl like that."

I'm going to be fucking sick again.

Was Miranda the girl?

Please *Jesus*, let Miranda not be that poor girl.

I masturbated to thoughts of that night and that video for *years*. Fucking years, even after I found out what a sociopath Bryce Gentry was.

It took a couple years but now she can't fucking cum without it. The pain.

And Miranda was with Bryce for two years. And most of the time, she needs pain to come. Oh Jesus. It was her. It was her, wasn't it. What sadistic shit did he do to her to make her not be able to cum without pain?

I think of everything she told me about her happy childhood in Ohio. Her mom and dad, still happily married after thirty-five years.

What the fuck did I think had happened to her to make her like sex the way she did? Why didn't I ever ask? Why didn't I demand to know?

I grab my hair and yank as hard as I can but it's not enough. I shout and run at the wall, slamming it with my fists.

I didn't want to know. I didn't want to know about the other men she'd been with. And I hoped, I don't know, maybe some people are just into pain. Maybe she didn't have to have demons in her past like I did.

But Bryce fucking Gentry?

Part of what was released in the Gentry files were videos of him *raping* women, multiple women, in the most *horrific* ways—

My fists go through the thin drywall and I kick and kick and kick at the boards underneath until Darren is pulling me backwards.

"Dylan!" he keeps shouting but I throw him off, turning on him.

"Was she the girl? That night, was she the girl? That we both…" Oh fuck, even beyond whatever Bryce did to her, there was what me and my own *brother* had—

Darren looks away and his voice is quiet as he admits, "Yeah. It was her."

I stomp to my desk and hurl my lamp against the wall but it's not enough. Not nearly fucking enough. I heave my entire desk onto its side, sending my monitor crashing to the floor. Still not fucking enough. I— *We*— Darren was at her mouth while she was trapped in that godawful leather hood and I— I—

I kick my fucking chair and then—

I can't fucking stand looking at my brother for one more second. I have to get out of here. Maybe if I run far enough, fast enough, I'll wake up from this fucking nightmare.

CHAPTER EIGHTEEN

MIRANDA

"Mmm." I lick my lips after I taste the pasta sauce. It's good. I followed the recipe online but you never know how those will turn out. Not that I'd really know. I don't cook that much. As in, never. I think this might be the second time I'm using this saucepan.

But I wanted to do something special for Dylan tonight.

I still feel like shit. He asked for honesty and I lied.

Lies of omission still count. I Googled it.

The water in the pot on the other boiler is finally boiling and I pour in the pasta, checking the box to see how long it's supposed to cook for.

I'm definitely taking up cooking, though. Having something to do with your hands when you're feeling lousy about stuff is turning out to be *very* useful. And I get the idea I'll be feeling lousy for a while because I'll have to keep lying to Dylan for who knows how long.

I sigh as I grab a wooden spoon and stir the noodles.

I'm about to put on the timer for nine minutes like the package said when there's a pounding on my front door.

I frown and look toward the door. I'm not expecting a package, I don't think. I set down the spoon and head for the door.

Looking through the peephole, I smile when I see it's Dylan. I unlock the door and pull it open.

"Dylan?" I exclaim. "What's wrong?"

I didn't get a good look at him through the warped fisheye lens but he's clearly upset. *Really* upset.

I reach out for him but he pushes past me into the house, dragging his hand roughly through his hair. I close the door and turn to find him pacing back and forth in the space behind the couches in my living room.

He looks terrible. I only saw him hours ago but somehow he looks like he's aged a decade.

"Dylan," my voice trembles. "What's going on? You're scaring me."

His eyes shoot to me and they're full of so much hurt a hole immediately punches through my chest.

"You dated Bryce Gentry." His voice is low and gravelly, like it hurts him to even get the words out.

I take a step backwards at the name, I can't help it.

"Is it true?"

My shoulders slump.

"Yes."

"Jesus," he breathes out and when I can bring myself to look back at him, it's like all the life has drained out of him. "You knew I knew him. You knew even before we started dating."

I nod and his jaw flexes.

"You knew I was there? That night?"

My eyes squeeze shut and my bottom lip trembles but I fight against the flood of tears choking their way up my throat.

"No. I didn't know that until later." I force my eyes open. He deserves the complete truth. "But I guess I always knew there was a possibility."

He drops to his knees, his face absolutely devastated.

"Why? Why would you—?" He shakes his head and for the first time, I see tears glistening at the edges of *his* eyes. "Then why would you even flirt with me that night at the conference? Why would you let me—?"

It's time. Time for the *whole truth.*

I suck in a breath but it still takes everything in me to keep my voice even remotely steady. "Bryce Gentry tried to break both of us. For a little while I tried to go back to being the girl I was before I met him. But there was no going back. So then I tried to be this other woman. The one everyone else sees from the outside. Confident. Unbreakable. *Perfect.* But I was *dying* on the inside because she was a lie, too."

I beg him with my eyes to understand. "So I went looking for..." I trail off, shaking my head. "A kindred spirit? I researched you. I went to talk to the woman they said that you'd—"

He flinches back in revulsion. "So you knew what I— You knew my fucking proclivities before I even came after you that night?"

I nod, my chin wobbling so hard I have to take another huge breath. "I honestly don't know if I was looking for someone to commiserate with or if I wanted someone else to– to hurt me and play the same fucked up games that Bryce used to."

I take a step closer but he jerks back.

"But what I found instead was *you.* I never— You were never— Please, Dylan, I'm so sorry."

He gets to his feet, holding onto the wall for strength.

"Wait, Dylan, please—don't go." I reach a hand toward him but he looks at it like it would burn him.

"You went looking for the monster," he says. "And that's what you found. Jesus, what I did to you that night." He drags his hands down his face, with his nails like he's trying to tear at his skin.

"You didn't do anything to me that I didn't want. You know I liked it. I wanted it rough."

"So did my mother!" he shouts. "She didn't leave either!"

I cry out at the accusation. It cuts. It cuts deep, him comparing me to the woman he never forgave.

His face is full of anguish as he backs away. "I already helped Bryce break you once. You only came back because of how deeply he scarred you. And instead of helping you heal, I've only been digging the knife in deeper. Keeping you broken, just like my father did my mom."

"No!" I swallow down my hurt and focus on what's important here. "You're a good man. It's your brother that's the monster."

"What?"

From the total confusion on his face, it's clear he still has no idea. But I'm done with secrets.

"After you left that day we had lunch at Darren's house, he threatened me. He said if I didn't convince you to take the contract with my company, he'd release a video of us he'd taken that first night at the garage. He's been having you followed. He wants you out of the company. Or at least out of the decision making. I think he might even be sabotaging your trials with the new processing chips somehow."

Dylan just shakes his head like he literally can't comprehend my words.

But if nothing else, I have to make him understand how dangerous his brother is.

"He hit me, Dylan. He punched me and kicked me and threatened worse." I lift my shirt to show him the bruises on my ribs. "Please don't trust him."

Dylan just keeps shaking his head as he stumbles backwards toward the front door.

"Wait, Dylan, please—" I follow him but he shoves an arm out and I stop.

"Please, Dylan," I plead. I'm shattering. Can't he see that being with him was the first time I've been whole ever since Bryce. With him I've been able to believe that I wasn't worthless. That I had so much value, I could change someone's whole life.

But now— Now—

"Dylan, no." I'm begging now and I don't even care. "I can't— Not without you."

But he's got his hand on the doorknob. He twists it and then wrenches the door open so hard, I'm shocked it's not ripped off its hinges.

And then he turns and disappears out into the pounding rain without another look back.

CHAPTER NINETEEN

DYLAN

"You're all wet, honey. But I bet I could warm you right up."

I glare up at the barely dressed girl leaning over me. "Did I ask for any fucking company?"

Her plastered on smile falters but only slightly. The strobe light from the front of the club flashes our way, illuminating just how much makeup she has caked on her face.

She disgusts me just like this entire place disgusts me. Which is exactly why I'm here. It's where I fucking belong.

"Leave," I order when she looks like she's going to make a second attempt. I don't want a fucking lap dance. I didn't come here for that.

"No," I say as she starts to turn away. I down the glass of whisky in front of me. "First have them bring me two more of these."

She nods and then scurries away.

I look around at the garish lights. At the girls dancing on poles. At the desperate men lining the catwalks waving cash. At the women grinding on men's laps in the dark.

This is a place for bottom feeders and perverts.

And monsters like me.

This is where I used to hunt, after all.

A lap dance can be bought for a nominal fee but for just a little more, a girl will go home with you. And for just a little more still, she'll let you do whatever you want to her.

Choke her. Slap her. Humiliate her. Gag her with your cock. Assfuck her. Be as rough as you fucking want.

Whatever sick shit gets you off.

Another girl shows up with two more glasses of whisky. She makes a big show of leaning over and showing her tits as she puts them on the table.

"Get the fuck out of my fucking face."

I take the first glass and down it. The fire in my throat fucking burns. It makes my eyes water but I reach for the second glass anyway.

Anything to numb today.

Anything to be numb.

Which is probably fucking stupid.

Now I know what I should have all along. Why have I fought it for so many years? It was inevitable. There was never any hope that Darren or I would turn out any other way. Not with him as our father.

And to think I thought I'd *protected* Darren.

Ha.

Just goes to show what a fucking fool I've been. Walking around thinking I'd made a difference, that any of us could fight against what he made us.

I shake my head and lift the glass to my lips. I don't down it. I decide to nurse this one. There's no hurry. I'll have the rest of my life to simmer in my own shit. Tonight is just the beginning of living with my eyes open.

And the first night of the rest of my life living without *her*.

My eyes close as pain sears through my stomach.

Motherfucker, I thought this shit was supposed to help make me fucking numb. I down the second glass after all and it burns only slightly less than the first.

But I still see her. On the floor after I knocked her down. Her eyes still pleading with me to stay.

To fucking *stay*.

Just like my mother.

How many times did I see Mom on the ground, crying after Dad hit her? After he *raped* her?

I'm fine, Dylan. Leave us alone. Don't try to get involved in things you don't understand.

Suddenly all the alcohol in my stomach isn't sitting well. I'm going to be fucking sick. The thought of me turning Miranda into my mother—

Fuck. I shove my chair back and head for the rest rooms but I'm not sure I'll make it there in time.

It doesn't help that now that I'm standing, I feel the effects of the alcohol far more than when I was sitting. It's hard to walk in a straight line and the flashing lights from the stage are piercing as I stumble in the direction of the bathrooms.

I'm almost there when I hear a commotion off to my left.

"No. No touching. Stop!"

At a table in a dark corner nearby, a dancer is struggling to get off a guy's lap. He's groping her tits with one hand and holding her down with the other while he dry humps her.

Son of a—

I stalk over to them.

"She said to let her go, you piece of shit."

I grab the hand of the arm he has around her waist and wrench it backwards until he lets out an effeminate cry and lets her go.

She springs out of his lap and hurries off.

"Who the fuck are you, asshole?"

It's only now as I look around the table that I realize the fucker assaulting the girl isn't alone. There's a whole table of douchebags—frat boys who haven't aged well—and they look pissed.

I grin at them and crack my knuckles.

"I'm the guy who calls out assholes and puts them in their place. Like your friend here. No means no, fuck face."

The biggest guy at the table shoves his chair back and gets in my face. "You wanna say that again, motherfucker?"

I lean in, "I said your friend is a pathetic asshole who has to force women at a strip club to get his rocks off because he can't get any anywhere else."

The thug shoves me so hard in the chest I stumble back a couple steps.

Oh hell yeah, fucker, let's fucking dance. My hand forms a fist and I come back swinging. I get one satisfying hit in, busting up the big bastard's face.

He comes back at me and sucker punches me in the gut.

I take it and laugh at the pain.

He thinks he can hurt me? After everything I went through today, he thinks a fucking punch can hurt me?

I swing again with all my might and all my fucking rage and all my fury. Hearing the cartilage of his nose break is so satisfying that I immediately swing again.

I guess that pisses off his buddies because more hits come at me from all sides. The whisky is finally doing its job, though. I'm fucking numb. I turn around and roar at the bastards and hit anyone and anything I can get my goddamned fists on.

CHAPTER TWENTY

MIRANDA

After Dylan stormed out earlier, I cried for about an hour. Then I cleaned up the burned spaghetti sauce. Then I kept cleaning. And cleaning. And cleaning.

I'm scrubbing the baseboards when I get Daniel's call.

"Are you watching the news?"

"The news?" I frown. "Who watches the news anymore?"

I hear his huff of frustration over the line. "Turn on your TV. Channel 4. Right now."

I drop the cloth I'm using and go over to the living room and grab my remote, flipping the TV on to Channel 4.

"Mark Morales, at Mercy hospital, has more on this breaking story," says the perky news reporter, right before the screen flips to a reporter standing beside the hospital bed of a guy who looks like he got beat up really badly.

That's when I read the ticker running at the bottom of the screen.

Tech billionaire Dylan Lennox, Lennox Brothers Corp, in jail tonight after bar brawl at a strip club leaves two hospitalized.

"Holy shit."

"Right?" Daniel agrees.

We both watch in silence.

"This is Mark Morales of KQYN. So let me just ask a few questions to set the stage. You and your buddies were at the Big Bottoms Gentleman's Club?"

The man in the hospital bed nods. "Just blowing off some steam on guy's night, ya know how it is."

It's a little hard to understand him because his jaw is swollen and his lip is split. His nose is obviously broken and there's a large white bandage circling his head, not to mention the black eye and what looks like a broken arm.

Holy shit, did Dylan really do all that?

"But then this guy just comes and jumps us. He must have been on something with as crazy as he was. He just starts wailing on my friend so I jumped in to try to protect him and the guy turns on me."

"Did you recognize the man as Dylan Lennox, tech billionaire?"

"Naw, man. It was dark in there. I just knew there was this guy like on meth or whatever, just savage. He was attacking us and I had to do whatever it took to keep my friend from getting killed."

My shoulders slump and I feel about ten inches tall.

"Miranda? You there?"

I startle at Daniel's voice. I'd forgotten he was on the phone.

God, I don't even want to answer because answering might lead to questions which would only lead to more questions, which would—

"Miran—"

"I'm here."

"Are you okay? Is Dylan violent? Has he ever hurt you or threaten—"

"No! God. He's not like that, okay? We got in a fight today and he was upset when he left, but he's not violent."

"Two guys in the hospital says different."

"He's not violent towards me. Towards women. There's a difference."

Daniel makes a noise like he's not convinced and I swipe a hand down my face. I don't have time to deal with Daniel right now.

"Look, thanks for calling me. This was really helpful and I really do appreciate it."

"But fuck off? Look, okay, I get it. I just worry about you. And if he ever hurts you, I'll cut his balls off and roast them for dinner."

"Wow, thanks for that image."

"You're welcome." There's a pause and then, "But seriously, babe. You okay?"

I sigh, muting the TV as the reporter continues to talk to the oaf in the hospital bed. "I will be."

I don't know if that's true but it's what Daniel needs to hear.

Long after Daniel hangs up and the news segment is over, I'm still trying to think of what to do.

Because something has to be done.

This is my fault. Dylan already had such skewed misconceptions about himself because of how his father raised him and the things he liked in bed. Then with what I revealed to him about Darren, on top of learning about me and Bryce and that night...

He has no support system right now. He's all alone in the world and I know better than anyone how desperate and terrifying a feeling that is.

Bryce made me feel helpless and worthless but over the last month with Dylan I've finally begun to believe it's not true. Together we were strong.

He's still the other half of me. Even if I've hurt him too much for him to ever be able to be with me—oh *God* even the thought chokes me and makes me want to fall to my knees and curl up in a ball, but I fight the impulse—even if he can never be with me, I'm still the only one who can help him right now.

He's still my heart and I'm his. So I'll help him in the only way I can think of. I'll fight for him when he can't fight for himself.

CHAPTER TWENTY-ONE

DYLAN

"You have a visitor," the guard says.

"I don't want to see them." I look back down to the book I'm reading. *Crime and Punishment*. Dostoyevsky seemed the only appropriate reading material.

The only people who'd want to visit me are Miranda, Darren, or the company lawyer. I'm not interested in seeing any of them.

There's a reason I didn't bother making a phone call to get bailed out. If there's anywhere I belong even more than a seedy strip club, it's gen pop at the Santa Clara County Jail.

"She said you'd say that," the beefy guard says. "She also said to tell you her name is Chloe Lennox."

My head shoots up and my book drops to the floor. "C-Chloe?"

"So you gonna see her?"

I nod and get to my feet.

But no, it can't be my sister. Not after all these years.

How would she even know I was in jail? Me getting locked up can't have made national headlines.

I've convinced myself it won't be her by the time I'm led into the visiting area. It has to be Miranda just using Chloe's name because she guesses I won't see her if she used her own name. I have half a mind to turn around in the last hallway the guard leads me down, I'm so sure I'm right.

But what if...? It's the tiniest doubt that keeps my feet moving forward. If there's even the slimmest possibility it actually is my sister waiting for me out there, I owe it to her to show my face.

My breaths get shorter as the guard swipes his keycard and then types in a number on a keypad to unlock a large metal door. There is a row of private booths partitioned off with glass separating inmates from visitors.

I desperately search every face we pass as he leads me down the aisle. But it's not until we get to the booth that's the third from the end that I see her.

"Chloe," I breathe out, hardly believing my eyes.

I tumble into the chair and then grab desperately for the phone. She already has hers up to her ear.

"Chloe. How are you— Why—" I have a thousand questions. A thousand things I want to say but now that she's here in front of me, I'm struck speechless.

She's so beautiful it hurts to look at her.

She has Mom's heart-shaped face and her curly auburn hair looks lighter, like she's been spending time in the sun.

And she looks somehow... I don't know. Grown up. Like she's a woman and not a girl.

But still so familiar it hurts. She still has a dusting of freckles scattered across the bridge of her nose and her cheeks. She's still the sister I teased all growing up. The sister I love more than anything in the world.

She smiles and lifts her hand to the glass, and tears glisten in her eyes.

"It's so good to see you," she says softly.

I lift my hand to meet hers and I blink hard, fighting back my own tears.

"I can't stand not being able to hug you," she says.

"I'll pay bail. I'll get out, okay?" I can't get the words out fast enough. "Tell them I'll pay bail. Right now. Go tell them right now."

She nods and stands up, swiping at her eyes.

The whole process takes a couple of hours and I'm kicking myself for not asking Chloe at least a few more questions while I had her there. Jesus, I didn't even ask her how she is. How she's been all these years. If she's okay.

She looked all right. Healthy, I mean. But maybe she was just putting on a front for my sake? Jesus, the first time she sees me in six years and I'm in fucking *jail*.

I only barely stop myself from snapping in impatience at the release officer who seems to be moving at a snail's pace in processing my paperwork to get my belongings back to me. But *finally*, I'm back in my own clothes and being led to the waiting area for friends and family.

When the officer opens the door and lets me through, I see her again.

And not just Chloe.

Miranda is sitting with her, holding her hand as she waits.

Of course.

Of course it was Miranda. That stubborn woman. What did she do? Get on a plane right after I left her house to track Chloe down in Austin and let her know what a fuck up her big brother had become? I've only been in lock-up for a little over a day.

But I don't even care, I'm so grateful to see my little sister.

I jog over to them and Chloe bounces to her feet. She throws her arms around my neck. I bury my face in her hair and hold her, lifting her up off the ground and swinging her back and forth.

"You're here," I breathe into her curly hair.

"I'm here," she says back, laughing and crying at the same time.

I hold her for a long time and when I finally let her down, she takes my hand. Her smile is pained now. "There's a lot we need to talk about." Her gaze flickers over to Miranda.

"There's a park not far from here. Why don't I drive you there so the two of you can talk. In private."

Chloe gives an appreciative nod, reaching out and squeezing Miranda's hand.

There seems to be an understanding between the two of them. And seeing the woman I love and the sister I've always adored connecting like this? I can't say it doesn't affect me.

Jesus, I thought I'd accepted my fate to live out the rest of my life as a miserable, lonely fuck. But now here they are, the two lights of my life, and I don't know— I don't know anything anymore.

We walk out to the parking lot in silence, Chloe's hand in mine. She squeezes every so often and looks up at me with a sunny smile.

The last two days have exhausted me and I feel scraped out on the inside. Empty of all the storming emotions that had me raging at the bar and screaming in my cell the first night.

That's not true, though.

I have one emotion left and it's so overwhelming I can't stop the tears that spring to my eyes.

Gratitude.

Gratitude to be here with my sister. Gratitude to Miranda for making this happen. Gratitude I didn't do something even stupider at the bar so I was able to get out of jail with nothing more than some money and paperwork. Gratitude to be fucking alive.

Chloe sits with me in the back seat while Miranda chauffeurs us the five minutes to a park. It's a small green space with trees and a green lawn where some kids are playing soccer. There's a little path through the trees that Chloe points out.

"I'll wait for you here," Miranda says, pulling an e-reader out of her purse.

I shoot her a grateful look and she just nods at me, her expression full of compassion and understanding. How can she? After how I treated her?

I turn away. Chloe takes my hand again as soon as we're out of the car.

"How have you been?"

I feel stupid as soon as I ask the question. It's so banal. Something a stranger might ask and it feels all wrong.

But Chloe just smiles up at me and squeezes my hand again. "Good. I've been *good*." But then a cloud covers her features. "It was hard at first, I won't lie. After everything that… happened. The first year especially."

I cringe. "I'm so sorry I didn't—"

She looks up at me. "It's okay. Miranda explained."

"She did?"

"You thought I blamed you?"

My breath catches and we walk several paces. "How could you not? I didn't see— Didn't realize what was happening even though I was—"

But she shakes her head. "Don't you get it? He was the master manipulator. No one ever saw him for what he was."

"But I did." I stop walking and look down at her. "We all saw what he did to Mom. I don't know why I never thought he'd do it to you, too. I just—"

But Chloe's shaking her head violently. "I know what you thought but you were wrong. It wasn't Dad."

My blood freezes in my veins at her words. "What… what do you mean?"

Her features are tight with pain and her face is pale. "It was Darren, not Dad. For years, it was Darren who would come into my room at night and… and hurt me."

Oh Jesus no.

All my equilibrium from the car is gone in an instant.

I stagger back into a tree and Chloe moves with me. Our hands separated when I moved so suddenly but she takes mine again.

"But I followed him," I whisper. "That day I came in. I went through your bathroom and found Dad—"

Her face is still pained as she explains, "You found Dad in his home office. Which he put in Darren's old room after he moved out and Dad had the heart attack. Dad always worked in his pajamas with those damn earphones on when he worked from home—remember how Darren gave them to all of us that Christmas, the noise cancelling kind? It was so Dad would never hear—"

She breaks off but I still don't understand.

She's quick to clarify. "Darren ran through the bathroom and was out the other door into the hallway before you ever got there. Dad had no idea about what was going on until he saw Darren run through the room. Then then you came in moments later screaming at him and beating him up."

I shake my head. "But— But then why didn't he say? Or fucking do something about it?"

Tears fall down her cheeks. "I think he might have threatened to once he connected the dots and realized what Darren had been doing."

I just stare at her, confused.

"And I think Darren killed him for it. Poisoned him and made it look like a heart attack."

I blink, horrified. "Why didn't you *tell me?*" To have carried all of this, by *herself*, after all the trauma she'd already been through at my brother's hands. She'd only been seventeen for God's sake.

"I was terrified he would kill you, too." She swipes at a tear. "So I never said. And then you two started the business together and I was so afraid. I was afraid all the time. I was so afraid of him, and you two were so close, I was afraid to contact you in case he found out and—"

"Oh God." I pull her into my arms and crush her tight to my chest. "Fuck, I'm so sorry, Chloe. I'm so fucking sorry I didn't realize."

She nods against my chest, crying, and I hold her. Jesus, all these years I had it wrong. I had it all so wrong. Chloe didn't blame me. She'd been afraid. And she was protecting *me*. How had all of this ended up so backwards?

Darren.

Darren was how all this had happened.

Miranda was right.

Maybe I wasn't a monster, and my father might be dead, but there's one devil still left breathing.

I pull back from my sister and run my thumbs underneath her eyes to wipe away her tears. "Shh, shh, it's all okay now. You never have to be afraid again. I swear it."

CHAPTER TWENTY-TWO

DYLAN

Darren pushes open the door to his seedy hotel in Thailand with a woman on his arm, a prostitute by the look of her. The astonishment is clear on his face when he sees me.

"Jesus, Dylan," he says, grabbing his chest. "You scared the shit out of me!" He laughs and shoos the woman off. "I'll see you another night, sweetheart."

She giggles but wobbles off in her four-inch plastic heels.

Darren turns back to me, a wide grin on his face. "What the hell are you doing here?" He strides forward and leans down to give me a big hug.

I'm sitting on a stained couch in a hotel room that I'd say has seen better days except that nope, I'm pretty sure this place has always been the roach-infested quarter-star accommodations that I see before me.

I clap him on the back, too.

When Darren pulls away, though, his brows are scrunched together. "Are you all right? The lawyers called and said you were in jail for brawling? I told Jenkins to bail you out immediately and I was flying home later tonight to make sure you were okay."

He looks so sincere. One hundred percent sincere. If I hadn't heard it from Chloe's own mouth, it might even be enough to make me question everything Miranda told me.

But I did hear it from Chloe and so I can only look on my brother and wonder how long I've lived with such a sociopath and not known it. Was he always this way or was he at one time genuinely the brother I loved?

"No worries," I say, holding out a glass of whisky. "We got it all sorted out. And a trip to Thailand sounded like exactly the kind of getaway I needed to escape all that shit back there. But brother, shit, couldn't you afford nicer digs?"

He takes the glass and laughs. "Right? I saw the place and thought the taxi-driver was shitting me. But then I thought, what the fuck, why not rough it like the locals for a night?"

Then his face goes sober. "But man, I'm sorry about that girl. I know you really liked her. It's just hard when you're as high profile and powerful as we are to trust people. Everybody has an angle. Everybody wants something."

I nod and take a sip of the glass I've been nursing for over an hour while I waited for him to come back. "Well now I know better."

I lift my glass. "To knowing better."

Darren clinks his glass with mine. "To knowing better."

We both drink. Darren downs his, laughing and making a face when the glass is empty. "Whooeee, that burns."

I laugh. "No kidding. You want some more?" I hold up the bottle.

"Hell yes."

I pour him another.

"Bitches aren't fucking worth it," I say, slurring my words. "Bros before hoes."

Then I raise my glass again. "Bros before hoes!"

He clinks his glass again, laughing at me and shouting, "Bros before hoes!"

We both down our glasses.

"Man I've missed this." He relaxes back in a plastic lounge chair beside me, the least offensive looking piece of furniture in the room. "Us just relaxing and hanging out. Now I sort of wished I hadn't sent the girl away cause the only thing that would make this better would be her sucking our dicks right now."

"Bros *plus* hoes?" I offer.

He laughs and nods.

I just shake my head though. "Women are too complicated. They're needy and whiny."

Darren pours himself some more whisky. "True enough."

He holds out the bottle to me but I raise a hand to decline. "I had half the bottle before you got here. Had to relax after that long ass flight. Remind me again why we made our factory in the middle of fuck all nowhere Asia?"

"Uh, cause the labor is cheap as shit? And the tax breaks are *sick*."

"And it doesn't hurt that you get to come over here once a quarter and do whatever you want to girls in some shithole rat-infested motel and no one's ever the wiser, huh?"

"What?" Darren looks confused, the smile dimming a notch on his face.

"Like that girl you were bringing back here." I sit up a little straighter. "You were gonna what? Rape her and beat her within an inch of her life? Cause that's what you get off on, right?"

Darren sits up in his chair, the smile finally dropping from his face. "What the hell are you talking about. She was a *prostitute*. You can't rape a prostitute. Jesus. You of all people should know that."

It's a well-aimed barb but it's not stopping me now that I'm on a role.

"Why else would you be staying in this shithole?" I gesture to the room around us, "instead of one of the nice international hotels? You want a place where no one will care about who comes and goes. And a place where no one will notice the disappearance of just another cheap whore."

"What the fuck, Dylan?"

Darren's whole face is red as he jumps to his feet, indignant.

"Her hair was the same color as Chloe's. Do you find ones that look like our sister on purpose, you sick fuck?"

Darren lunges for me but he stumbles after the first step and falls to his knees. He blinks and shakes his head, looking up at me with unfocused eyes. "Wha— you do to-me?" he asks sluggishly.

"What?" I ask calmly. "I thought you liked to party. Chloe told me this is how you did it to her at the beginning so she couldn't fight back. She was just fourteen at the time, wasn't she?"

I calmly stand up, taking with me the little tin box that I bought before getting in the private jet. You really can find anything on the streets of San Francisco.

But before I pull the lid off the tin, I pull the gloves out of my pocket and tug them on. Then I open the tin and fill the needle with the yellow liquid in the vial.

Darren tries to get to his feet but only falls back down again. I didn't scrimp on the dosage of GHB I put in the whisky bottle.

I kick him in the ribs and he doubles over so I kick him in the back to get him straightened back out.

Then I drop on top of him and yank his arm out, positioning the needle at the fattest vein.

He just starts laughing.

"She always was the best fuck. You've never known a tight cunt until you fuck our little sister. You should try it."

I believed Chloe and Miranda. I did. But still, seeing the true face of my brother for the first time...

"She'd always cry when I snuck in her room at night to fuck her. You would've loved it."

My jaw tightens so hard I swear my teeth are going to crack. I know what he's doing. Trying to rile me so I won't inject him, or maybe so I'll hit him instead and leave some DNA behind so this won't just look like the tidy overdose I intend.

But I have something that my brother never understood.

Discipline.

So I shove the needle in his arm and root around until I hit the vein. Then I depress the plunger.

"You're just like me," he shouts. "You like it when they scream. Nothing makes you harder than when they fight you and you get to hurt them anyway. You love being a god just as much as I do, brother. We're both our father's son! We're both—"

He cuts off mid-sentence and his mouth shuts and then gapes open, shuts and opens as his eyes go distant.

I move off him and sit beside the brother I loved my whole life and watch as the life drains from his eyes.

EPILOGUE

MIRANDA

Things have been quiet since Dylan came back from Thailand. Quiet but good. We spend every night together in each other's arms.

He hasn't told me exactly what happened but I read online about how his brother supposedly OD'd during his trip to Thailand.

No one knows Dylan was there. He traveled by private jet and apparently bribed whatever local officials needed bribing. He told me that much so I wouldn't worry.

There was a funeral for his brother that he arranged and went to and looked appropriately grieved at. I couldn't quite bring myself to go but I saw pictures. When I asked him later he said he *was* grieving. Grieving for the brother he'd lost, even if that person had never been real.

But he didn't grieve for long, because while he'd lost a fictional brother, he'd gained back a very real sister.

Chloe had extended her visit and only gone back home to Austin a couple of days ago. Dylan became a different person with her around. He lit up, teasing her and joking with her. I could see what it must have been like with them growing up together. It was clear Chloe idolized him. I was so happy for him, having that.

At night though, he still had nightmares.

I woke him as gently as possible, and now, finally, he didn't turn me away. He let me hold him. The last barriers between us were finally crumbling.

We made love every night, sometimes in the mornings, too. I think Dylan will always need that with me—it's like it's the only way I can communicate with him that I really love him and trust him. With my body.

We haven't played since that awful night in the alley.

The love-making is wonderful and I'll be more than fulfilled if it's all we ever have. But what I don't like is the thought that Dylan is closing off a part of himself in order to be with me.

I hate the thought that he still believes any part of himself is monstrous. I still see it in his eyes sometimes, though. The self-loathing. Not as often anymore but it's still there.

And it's time once and for all for him to accept every part of himself as good and whole and wonderful.

We were headed out on a date tonight and I was going to tell him all of this, but then I got a fucking flat tire.

So now I'm stranded out on an abandoned backroad at nine-thirty with no cell-service. Frickin' awesome.

I've been looking for cars to flag down but I swear no one drives on this piddly little road my GPS directed me down on.

I keep my eye on my rearview mirror.

And finally, finally, I see headlights coming my way. I wait until the car parks behind mine and a man steps out. His lights are still on so he's a tall, dark silhouette as he approaches.

My heartbeat starts to ramp up.

Even though I know he's coming, I still jump when he raps on my window. I roll it down.

"Do you need help, miss?"

"I- I've got a flat and don't have a spare in the trunk."

"I'm happy to help. Just step on out. I've got the gear in my van back here."

I bite my bottom lip nervously. "Are you sure?" I look up and down the road.

"Done it a hundred times. I just need a little help getting the jack in place. We'll get you back on the road in no time."

I glance up and down the road again. "Okay. Thanks. My cell phone doesn't have any bars or I would have called triple A or my boyfriend."

I open the door and step out. My heels and glittery halter dress aren't exactly tire-changing attire but I hope I can be of some help.

"This way," he says, gesturing me toward his van.

I rub my arms, trying to stay warm in the chilly night air. "I'll just wait here while you get the jack."

"Did I tell you to wait here?"

Suddenly the cadence of the man's voice has completely changed, from friendly to harsh. "I told you to come with me to the fucking van."

Oh shit.

I try to run back to my car and the open door but he snatches me from behind around the waist.

I start to scream but he clamps a hand over my mouth. It's only seconds later that I'm being shoved in the van. He holds me down with his knees while he pulls the van door shut behind him.

Trapping me in.

Oh God, he's got me trapped.

He wastes no time, either.

"That mouth's so pretty," he pants, straddling my body and scooting until his knees hold down my shoulders, his groin right in my face.

The next thing I know he has his cock out.

"You want this, don't you, slut? I fuckin' know you do. Saw it in your eyes you were begging for it right when I came up to you in your car. So now you're gonna fuckin' take it and take it all the way down your throat."

"No!" I scream but he pinches my nose so the only way I can breathe is by gasping, mouth open.

He takes advantage and shoves his cock in, so far back that I choke.

"That's right. Oh fuck, yeah. Choke on it." He shoves it even further, down my throat until I gag. Tears pour down my cheeks as I choke and gag around his cock.

He pulls out and I gasp for air but it's only a momentary reprieve because the next second he's shoving it right back down again.

I writhe underneath him, squirming and trying to shove him off but it's no use, he's too big.

I don't know how long he fucks my face for, long, agonizing minutes but finally he pulls out. I gag and choke in air, turning on my side. He gets up off me and I try to take my chance and scramble for the door.

He grabs my ankle right before I can grab the handle, though, and yanks me roughly backwards.

"Oh, I ain't done with you, pretty girl. Not by a fuckin' long shot."

I screech as he shoves me on my back and rips my skirt up. He roughly yanks my thong down and shoves my legs up to my chest.

I know what comes next. My pussy is completely exposed to him and I cry when I feel him line up and shove inside me.

"You're wet for it, bitch." He slaps my ass so hard I know I'll feel it every time I sit down tomorrow. "You're so fucking wet for it."

I weep harder, shoving at him uselessly with my hands.

He's too big.

Too strong.

He laughs at my struggles and just keeps fucking me ruthlessly. With hard, slamming thrusts that drive my back into the industrial carpet of the van's floor. The beading on my gown digs into my back.

"Wanna see them titties. Them fancy titties you hiding away in that fancy fuck dress."

He reaches down and grabs the front of my dress in both hands and rips it in two. It had a built in bra so now I'm completely exposed to him.

"No!" I cry as he reaches for my breasts. He pinches one nipple, grabbing it and twisting it so hard I scream.

He bows low over me and bites my bottom lip as his hips continue to pound me. "Cry for me." He grabs my hair and yanks my head back while he continues twisting the first nipple. "Fucking cry for me!"

The pain is excruciating. I feel him everywhere. He's everywhere. He's everything.

I couldn't possibly feel more.

But I'm wrong.

Oh God, I'm so wrong.

Because his hand slides down from my hair to my throat.

Our eyes meet and hold. I suck in a quick breath.

And then he starts to squeeze.

He's choking me.

And it's the most erotic thing I've ever fucking experienced.

The fact that he's allowing himself to go *this* far, that he's freeing himself *this* much, that he trusts me and trusts *himself* with me.

I am so in love with Dylan Lennox.

As his hand cinches tighter around my neck and I feel his command in every flex and sinew of his powerful body over me, the orgasm rises like a tsunami.

He sees it—he knows me perfectly—and he releases both my throat and his iron grip on my nipple and the rush of oxygen and sensation— Oh God, I—

I wail as I come and clench around every part of his body I can get at.

I love him, love him, *love him*—

Light bursts and sensation rushes outward from my center. Oh— *Oh*—

Dylan's lips smash down on me and I feel his cum spurt deep inside me. So fucking deep, uniting us, making us one.

I ride the heavens with him by my side. Always by my side.

When the wave crests and dissipates, I find myself in his arms as he strokes my hair gently back from my face.

"You're so beautiful," he whispers. "So fucking perfect. The most beautiful, perfect thing that God ever created on this earth."

I laugh and bury my face against his chest.

"I don't think we're going to make it to the restaurant."

"Fuck the restaurant."

I giggle and wrap my arm around him, wanting to be as close to him as possible without having him inside me.

"The van was a nice touch." I look around us. "Where did you even get it?"

"I was at work when I got your text, so I borrowed it from maintenance."

"Thank you for coming," I whisper.

He guffaws. "Didn't have a whole lot of choice with you squeezing and spasming all over my cock like that."

I smack his chest. "That's not what I meant."

He laughs and grabs my hand, bringing it to his mouth and kissing my knuckles. "I know, babe. I know."

I wasn't sure how he'd respond to the text I sent half an hour ago with my location and the message:

Flat tire. Damsel in distress. Don't you dare be fucking ashamed. Let's play, baby.

"I love all of you, you know that? Your sweet side, your rough side. All of you."

He turns over on his side, propping himself up on his elbow and looking at me, the only light from the small overhead van light.

"You mean that?"

I nod vigorously. "Of course I do. I love you."

He stares at me a second longer. "Then I better lock this shit down. At least that's the way Chloe put it before she left on Tuesday."

He twists and reaches behind him and my eyes widen in shock when I see what he has in his hand when he turns back to me.

"You're shitting me."

A grin splits his face. "I am most certainly not shitting you. Miranda Marie Rose, will you do me the great honor of becoming my wife?"

I lift my hands to his cheeks. I swear I can't breathe. My eyes can't stop shooting from the diamond ring to Dylan's face, then back to the ring and then back to his face.

"Are you serious?"

He looks concerned. "Of course I'm serious. Jesus, Miranda. How did you not see this coming? I love you. You've changed my entire life. Changed *me*."

He sits up and helps me sit up too, then cups my face. "Be my wife. Make my happiness complete."

Tears spill down my cheeks and I nod, over and over again I nod because I'm not sure I could voice any actual words in this moment.

He grabs my hand and fits the ring onto the fourth finger of my left hand like he's eager to do it before I change my mind. Ridiculous man.

I throw my arms around him. "I fucking love you, do you know that?" I cry, so happy, so incredibly happy.

He pulls back from me and grins, then tugs me forward and kisses one cheek, then the other. "I always did love your tears."

Haven't read the first two books in the Break So Soft Series yet? Miranda isn't the only woman Bryce Gentry tried to break, she was just the first. Read Callie and Jackson's story in Cut So Deep and Break So Soft for a story of resilience, heartbreak, but above all, true love.

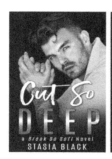 

Want to read an EXCLUSIVE, FREE NOVEL, Daddy's Sweet Girl, a dark stepfamily love story that is available only to my newsletter subscribers, along with news about upcoming releases, sales, exclusive giveaways, and more?

Get it here:
BookHip.com/MGTKPK

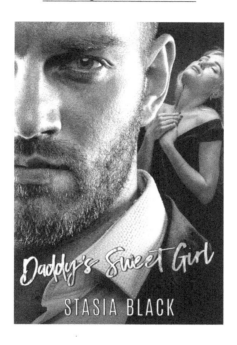

ALSO BY STASIA BLACK

MARRIAGE RAFFLE SERIES

Theirs to Protect

Theirs to Pleasure

Their Bride

Theirs to Defy

STUD RANCH STANDALONE SERIES

The Virgin and the Beast: a Beauty and the Beast Tale (prequel)

Hunter: a Snow White Romance

The Virgin Next Door: a Ménage Romance

BREAK SO SOFT SERIES

Cut So Deep

Break So Soft

Hurt So Good

Love So Dark (Coming Soon)

ACKNOWLEDGMENTS

I'm the kind of nerd who always reads the Acknowledgements page because I like a sneak peek into the behind the scenes. This book was really, really *fun* to write. Maybe because it was unexpected, I just had the idea, then wrote it in a mad two-week dash. And obviously all I had was sex on the brain during those two weeks which is why there's so much sex in the book, LMAO!

Anyway, on to the amazing people who helped help me every day. You guys keep this boat afloat because I would seriously sink without you!!!

Aimee B. – Epic hugs or our 2 year anniversary of knowing each other and for your fabulous, FABULOUS beta-reading magic :)

Alana A. – Gaaaaaah! You gave me the kick in the pants I needed in the 11th hour telling me, wait, this moment doesn't feel earned, which led to me writing like an extra $1/6^{th}$ of the book and giving so much more depth to the characters. Thank you!

Lisa L. – Thanks also for helping with the last minute read and your notes! You also helped me make the characters more rounded which was exactly what I needed. Thanks!!

To my assistants, Melissa P., Melissa L., and Jenn R., talk about keeping the boat afloat, geez, I seriously can't think of managing to put the number of books I'm able to without you gorgeous gals taking care of everything else so I can just write, write, write. *mwah*

Thanks to my hubby, though he never reads these, lmao. He's so damn cute, I'm watching him right now as he works away at his laptop. He's seriously the cutest damn nerd out there, folks, and I'm damn hashtag blessed that he's mine :)

ABOUT THE AUTHOR

Stasia grew up in Texas, recently spent a freezing five-year stint in Minnesota, and now is happily planted in sunny California, which she will never, ever leave.

She loves writing, reading, listening to podcasts, and has recently taken up biking after a twenty-year sabbatical (and has the bumps and bruises to prove it). She lives with her own personal cheerleader, aka, her handsome husband, and their teenage son. Wow. Typing that makes her feel old. And writing about herself in the third person makes her feel a little like a nutjob, but ahem! Where were we?

Stasia's drawn to romantic stories that don't take the easy way out. She wants to see beneath people's veneer and poke into their dark places, their twisted motives, and their deepest desires. Basically, she wants to create characters that make readers alternately laugh, cry ugly tears, want to toss their kindles across the room, and then declare they have a new FBB (forever book boyfriend).

Made in the USA
Coppell, TX
29 October 2020